THE CLARRINGTON HERITAGE

When Marise Dering marries Ben Clarrington and moves into the old mansion where the rest of the Clarringtons live, she's ordered to keep out of the closed-off sections of the third floor — but is not told why. It is only later that she learns the sinister family secrets . . . but has she been told all of them? As the family members begin perishing in odd and horrifying circumstances, Marise must try to uncover all the secrets of the Clarrington heritage . . .

ARDATH MAYHAR

THE
CLARRINGTON
HERITAGE

Complete and Unabridged

LINFORD
Leicester

First published in Great Britain

First Linford Edition
published 2013

A catalogue record for this book is available
from the British Library.

ISBN 978–1–4448–1799–7

Published by
F. A. Thorpe (Publishing)
Anstey, Leicestershire

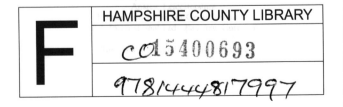

1

The watcher no longer took the trouble to hide behind the big crêpe myrtles across the street from the house. Now he stood at the edge of the time-broken sidewalk, staring openly at the fence and the gate and the windows and roofs peering over that barrier.

He knew that no chance passerby could see what he found so fascinating about the cut granite house. It was only one of the huge, obsolete mansions lining the street, in this neighborhood that now waited for the wrecking crews to smooth the solid walls away to make way for parking lots or MacDonald's fast food places.

The watcher's knowing eyes saw things invisible to the uninterested. No sign of decay marked the visible paintwork. The iron fence that led up in spear peaks to the stone steps showed no gaps. There was no broken glass in the windows, though small boys had broken those of

1

every other empty mansion on the block. Those tall narrow windows, protected in the upper stories by grillwork shutters, were intact and secretive. The house looked as if it had been caught in some eddy in time, unchanging and unchangeable.

The man had watched for over a week. Not once had he seen any sign of life inside the house, though once a boy came with a lawnmower, let himself in at the iron gate leading into the rear gardens, and spent a day mowing that invisible lawn. He had been the only living being visible in all those days.

No face looked from any of the heavily curtained windows. No hand reached out of the front door to explore the mailbox for letters.

No eyes, he was certain, had detected his presence. He sighed. He was going to have to do this the hard way.

★   ★   ★

The hallway was dark, but Marise found her way down the stair with practiced ease. A decade of prowling about the twilit house had trained her eyes to see in darkness. Though she knew it was eccentric (and she constantly scanned her consciousness for signs of madness), she felt somehow more secure when she was half hidden in shadows.

The entry hall loomed about her, a cavern of dimness and shadowy shapes. The grandfather clock ticked heavily and she caught her breath, her hand at her throat, feeling her heart pounding in time with its strokes.

No matter how often she stopped that pendulum, it always managed to swing enough to begin its ponderous ticking again. The mechanism was a mystery to her, for it was certainly not the weight-driven kind she understood. It was never wound, yet it continued to run, year after year, no matter how often she tried to stay the pendulum.

Nevertheless, she polished the finely carved wooden case and turned away, dust cloth in hand, to begin shining the panels of the front door. That deep tick had greeted her the first time she entered this house. The door itself had confronted her with its dark African wood, carved with monkeys and lions peering from a stiff-leafed forest.

Her first glimpse of it, as she mounted the steps beside Ben, had shocked her. Rightly or wrongly, she felt that a fortune built on slave trading should have avoided any reminder of Africa.

She remembered looking up at Ben inquiringly. He was staring down with such an eager expression that she forgot her objection to the door. Instead of speaking, she reached up to kiss him, just once, before entering the house where she would become one of his family, the Clarringtons.

She had stood there, waiting for the massive door to open, for the family to greet the bride and bridegroom, but that had not happened. At last Ben used his key.

There was nobody in the hall. The vaulted space above the entry was filled with shadows, the stair curving upward into dimness. Only the clock spoke, and its voice was not reassuring. There seemed to be no living soul at home.

Ben was pale in the varicolored light coming through the stained glass panels on either side of the door. His lips thinned against his teeth and he looked, for a moment, quite unlike the man she had just married. He seemed . . . different. Dangerous.

Marise closed her eyes and leaned against the door. She listened to the echo of Ben's voice as he called, trying to rouse at least one of his kin.

She'd smiled up at him. 'Don't look so grim! We gave them too little time, and it's possible the telegram never got here. Then again, they may have been out of town.'

His arm had been hard beneath her calming hand. 'People do like to acquire new in-laws gradually and in slow stages,' she added. 'This is a *fait accompli*, done before they have had time to react.'

The tight lines of his face relaxed a bit. 'You're right. You always have been, so far, and I'm alive to prove it. If I have you, I can do without anyone else, if I have to. Come here, and look into my magic mirror.'

'Magic?' she asked. In response he led her over the velvety carpet toward a towering hall tree, which was hung with an array of outdated hats and umbrellas. It had a chair seat and a drawer beneath that for miscellany. A long mirror was set in its back.

This was evidently very old, for the silvering had faded in fine lines and whorls. Her reflection seemed misty and undefined as she leaned to peer into the glass, her face that of a stranger in the alien mirror.

'Why it *is* magic!' she said, laughing with delight. Her face stared out as if from a place of crystalline ferns and unlikely flowers. The softening effect caused the sharp angles of her face, her fragile blonde looks, to become mystical and lyrical, instead of brittle.

'It makes me look almost pretty!'

Ben turned her to face him, hands on her shoulders. 'You *are* beautiful to me. I don't quite know how to explain this without making my people seem cold and uncaring. Really, they're not, but you're the first person in my life to make me feel warm inside. Loved.

'Besides, you kept me alive, brought me back from the edge of death when everyone else gave up on me. How could I possibly get along without you? You're the most nearly perfect thing I've ever found, so don't let me hear you say you're not pretty!'

He pushed her down gently onto the velvet seat of the hall tree. 'Now wait here while I run up to see where they've put us . . . if they got my message and put us anyplace at all. If they haven't, I'll choose for myself. My old room isn't what I want for our honeymoon. I used to stuff birds and collect rocks!' He smiled and tossed his coat and hat over the newel post. Then he bounded upward, two steps at a time.

She stared after him, feeling somewhat anxious. He'd seemed quite well for weeks now, but it was such a short time since his illness, something that even the best doctors hadn't been able to diagnose, she felt it would be wise for him to take things easy for a long time.

Then she smiled. They'd been married for three days . . . and nights. She had no reason to doubt his vigor, if nothing else.

'Marise Dering Clarrington, you are a worrier. Relax and be happy!' she ordered herself aloud.

A voice, so faint that afterward she was not totally certain she had heard it at all, quavered through the dimness of the hall. 'Happy? Happy? In this house?' She thought a peal of laughter, faint and ghostly, had followed those words.

Now, she knew that had been the first warning, the foreshadowing, of what she felt certain must be her own madness. But then she had clenched her hands in her lap. She was a practical country girl, and she did not hear voices where there was nobody to speak.

She was here, safe in Ben's home. Her nerves must be playing tricks after the long strain of nursing him. Their fast-paced courtship and swift marriage might easily have left her tense and fanciful.

She took a deep breath and relaxed. The sound of Ben's steps on the stair brought a smile to her face, and she rose and went to the foot of the steps to meet him.

'Well, do we have a place to lay our heads?' she called up to him.

The words died on her lips. Ben's face showed a fury she had never seen before. He reached down to take her hand and even through his fingers she could feel the racing of his pulse.

'They must not be here,' he said, and she knew he was lying. 'I've chosen to put us up in the tower rooms. That will be best. It's private and nobody will bother us.' His smile was more of a grimace.

'Anything you like, dear,' she said. 'But slow down. You have to remember that you've been sick. Now, lead the way. At least we can take the hand luggage up. Are there no servants? I'd have thought that in a house this large you would need several, to keep things going. Somebody needs to bring in my big trunk or your bride will be limited to wearing this one suit and pair of shoes.' She tried to sound teasing and cheerful, but she knew it didn't quite come off.

'Of course,' Ben responded. 'There's a couple who have worked for us forever. Hildy will be in the kitchen and I should have gone down to check with her the first thing. Andy, her husband, does all the heavy work. He's probably down in their quarters in the basement. I'll go get him.' His expression had lost the fury that had marked it. 'You go ahead with the little case. Straight up, around the first landing, then up the next flight. There's another landing after that, and halfway up that third flight you'll find a door on your right. It's in a sort of pie-shaped niche, and it leads to the tower rooms.'

Marise nodded. Taking up the case, she started up the lovely old stairway, curving around the side of the entry hall to the first landing. Ornate fixtures lit it, and the plum-colored carpet was soft underfoot. At the landing the corridor leading onto the second floor caught her attention. Muted lights in fixtures shaped like bunches of flowers illuminated a row of arched doors, one of which stood open.

Was someone there? She moved silently into the corridor and along it to the open doorway. The room beyond was empty of a tenant, although it was furnished. Or had been.

A rose-hung tester bed centered the farther wall, its hangings ripped from their supports, lying over it in tatters. Draperies patterned with roses of a matching hue were slashed and torn from the poles that had held them. The gray and rose carpet was smeared with what had to be dog dung. Fresh roses and shards of broken crystal vases lay amid the mess and the stench.

Someone had prepared this lovely room for the newlyweds. Someone else had torn it apart and fouled it past repair.

She put a hand over her nose and fled toward the stair. She ran up the remaining steps and into a small arched door leading to the tower.

She surmised that the ruined room was what had caused Ben's anger. If the door hadn't been ajar, if she had not yielded to the temptation to snoop, she would never have known that someone here must resent her enough to do this insane thing. Ben had lied to spare her feelings, and it was only her own folly that had wasted his effort.

Her heart thumped as she entered a

round room furnished as a sitting room. A short flight of stairs curved against one wall, leading, she understood at once, to a bedroom above. Though the furnishings were somewhat faded, the hangings slightly dusty, it was a charming room, full of light, for continuous windows circled it.

The tower, unlike any she had ever seen, was set into the rear of the house, looking over well-kept gardens. Even late fall had not robbed those of their charm, for chrysanthemums glowed in shades of bronze and gold amid the dark green leaves of evergreens.

Marise sat in a low rocking chair, her case at her feet, and there she had come to terms with the devastation she had seen in that pink bedroom. She loved Ben more than anything or anyone else. Nothing anyone in this hostile house did could drive her away. She'd stay, as long as Ben needed and wanted her.

Standing now in the same dim entry hall, a much older Marise opened her eyes and straightened her back. How little one knows, she thought, when one is young and in love, of what may come of your rashly given vows.

She gave the door a last polish with her cloth and shook her head. Behind every door in this place of many doors lay bits and pieces of her past. Each time she entered a room, some scene, happy or tragic or funny or horrifying, lay there in wait for her. It was terrifying, in a way, and yet she made a point of entering every room in the house on a regular basis.

Not every day; the human mind and spirit can bear only so much. But often enough to know that she had not lost her courage. Often enough.

She wondered how many times that might be, since she had barricaded herself and her doubts of her own mind's stability into Clarrington House. Of the large family that had lived and laughed and quarreled there, she was the sole survivor, and for ten years she had lived alone with her memories and her fears.

2

Of all the doors in the house, the one that opened into the parlor was the only one leading into untainted happiness. Marise always cleaned that room first, when she began tending the house. She might be mad, but she was not going to become dirty as well.

Now she pushed her cart of cleaning things to one side and fumbled in her pocket for the key to the double-leaved door. Even as she pushed it into the lock, she paused, remembering . . .

It had been, at least partly, the way Marise had speculated it might be. Their telegram, sent hastily as they set out for Channing and Ben's home, had arrived when most of the family was away.

Father Clarrington, the nurse, and Aunt Lina had taken Mother Clarrington to the Mayo Clinic for extensive tests, leaving only Hannibal, Ben's brother, there with Hildy and her husband. But

Hannibal had been called to the state capital, where he had a case before the State Supreme Court.

The telegram reached only Hildy. The cook had, Marise now knew, prepared the lovely room on the second floor for the newlyweds, ordering fresh flowers, cleaning everything spotlessly. That had been lovingly done, for Hildy was as much a part of the family as those born into it.

One question plagued Marise, as she made ready to meet her new family, who had, on their return, assembled in the parlor to greet Ben and his new wife. Who had destroyed that room?

Only the servants were in the house, and Hildy had been the one to make ready the bridal chamber. The rest of the family was gone, provably absent. This was not a house into which any chance prowler or vagrant could possibly find a way without leaving distinct traces of breaking and entering.

The solid front door was always locked, and that lock was not as old-fashioned as the house. The iron fence ran all the way around the five enclosed acres of gardens and grounds. The front, back, and side gates were locked, and the spear points topping the barrier were not merely ornamental. They would be dangerous to anyone trying to climb over.

Who could possibly have done violence to that room she had been meant to share with Ben?

But she had not been intended to see it . . . not after Ben knew what had happened there. She could never ask him or anyone else, without betraying the fact that she had seen. Over the years, she had worried over the question, wondering without knowing.

But on that first day after the rest of the family came she had inspected her makeup, fastened the modest pearl clips at her ears, and stood back to make sure.

The new dress, her first designer gown, fell in the same elegant lines she remembered from the fitting room. She wanted to look wonderful for her new in-laws, even though she knew she was not beautiful, except in Ben's eyes.

He was waiting for her in the sitting room. The way his eyes lit up as she floated down the six steps to join him told her that she had done her work well.

'Never let anybody tell you that you're not gorgeous!' he said, taking her hands and squeezing them lightly. 'I'd hug the stuffing out of you, but I'm afraid I'd mess you up, and you look wonderful.'

'Is my hair smooth at the back? It's hard to tell, even with the triple mirrors. I don't want it glued-looking.' She turned so he could see.

She felt his fingers touch the elaborate knot of curls that she had labored to erect and stabilize.

'Just ... exactly ... elegant!' he breathed into her ear. 'I can hardly wait to mess it all up tonight.'

She giggled. 'We'd better go down right now, or you'll mess it up anyway, and it took me hours to get it just right.'

They went down the broad staircase, hand in hand. Hildy, peeping through the curtain covering the open doors to the dining room, beamed at them and threw Ben a kiss from her wrinkled hand. Marise felt warmed by the old cook's friendliness. She had done her best to fill

17

the gap until the family arrived, and her good will had helped to ease any distress the newcomer had felt.

They paused at the parlor door. 'I love you,' Ben whispered in her ear. 'They will love you too. Don't be nervous. They're great people.'

But she had been terribly, frantically nervous, as the heavy doors opened wide.

She knew at once that the big man who pushed back the wooden panels had to be Hannibal. Though he was older, heavier, somehow tougher-looking than Ben, he was so like him that she felt an immediate kinship. He was beaming down at her with such honest delight that she felt her tension ease and the beginning of warmth steal into her cold hands.

'So you are the young lady who saved my brother's life,' he boomed. Her hand was swallowed in his immense paw, which seemed to radiate confidence and warmth. 'You're such a frail-looking child it seems strange, your rescuing someone from death. But Ben says you just refused to give up and made him pull himself through, even when the doctors couldn't decide what to do next. We owe you a big one, Marise. Welcome to the family!'

Her stiff smile softened and became real as she looked up at her brother-in-law. 'Don't be fooled by appearances, Hannibal. I'm a good, tough peasant to my toenails. I helped my brother and my father farm until they died and left the farm to me. I tried going it alone, but it was too much, so I sold the place and went into nursing. I do miss having good dirt to grub around in sometimes, but nursing is almost as good. If you can't grow things, why, making people well is a fine substitute.'

He laughed and pulled her into the room, where she could see several people waiting. 'This is your new father, Emanuel. All of the hardest heads in the family can be blamed on him, I'm afraid. But he's a sweetheart, just the same.'

The nearest of the family, a tall, slender old man, rose to meet her. Though his face was pale and ascetic-looking, his eyes were Ben's own black ones. Now they were inspecting her so sharply that she wondered if he might be angry to find this intruder in his household.

When he smiled, she was reassured. 'We have — no daughter.' He paused a moment, his eyes watering. 'We need one. Welcome, dear child. I only regret that as things worked out there was no one here to welcome you in person when you arrived. But we'll do everything we can to make up for that, rest assured. Come and meet your new mother.'

Ben had told her earlier that his mother asked to be brought down from what they called the hospital suite for the occasion. She looked fragile but lovely, her iron gray hair carefully done. Her makeup, however, couldn't hide her deathly pallor, and the nurse in Marise knew that she was in pain.

Marise knelt beside the electric wheelchair and looked up into the woman's pale eyes, which were totally unlike those of both her sons. Mother Clarrington looked deeply into her eyes, as her husband had done, as if searching for something, fearful of finding it. The sadness of her gaze warmed as she smiled at last.

The thin hand reached to grip her shoulder with surprising strength. 'I can see it,' said Mother Clarrington. 'You are good for Ben. He is more relaxed, happier than I have ever seen him. We are more than grateful, my dear, for your care of him. I must confess I was afraid, when we heard of your sudden marriage, that some gorgeous hussy had taken advantage of his weakened condition. Once I saw him, this morning, I knew the truth. You saved him when we were all bound by our own illness and responsibilities and could not even be beside him. Be happy, my dear.'

She sighed deeply and made a gesture with one frail hand. The stocky little nurse came forward as she said, 'Forgive me. I must leave you now. Edenson!'

The nurse was at her side at once. Marise smiled at her. 'Miss Edenson, if you need a day off sometime, just let me know. I will gladly look after Mrs. Clarrington. I am fully qualified, and I understand how confining it can be to have a patient who needs round-the-clock care.'

The woman's steely eyes glinted at her

with something like resentment. 'I am able to care for Mrs. Clarrington quite adequately without help,' she said in a brusque tone. 'But thank you.' There was no gratitude in her expression as she opened the big doors.

Mother Clarrington looked up as Marise rose from her knees to stand beside her. There was apology in her glance; then she turned her chair and trundled away to the small elevator let into the wall behind a tapestry near the stair.

As she watched the elevator door close, she felt a strong hand grasp her elbow. 'I'm Ben's Aunt Lina,' a gruff voice said.

Marise turned to meet the last member of the family. 'Ben has talked about you so much!' She reached to hug the old woman. 'He says you raised him because his mother was unable to. He was lucky to have you, with her so ill all through his childhood.' The scent of sandalwood wafted from Aunt Lina's sweater as she put her arms about the woman's shoulders.

Aunt Lina returned the hug awkwardly,

as if she were unused to demonstrations of affection. Her furrowed features relaxed, and the startling jade green eyes examined Marise closely. As had been true with every member of this odd family, it seemed that she was looking for something specific, something indefinable. Perhaps something menacing?

Marise felt that anyone as small as she could hardly be a menace to anyone, and Aunt Lina seemed to decide the same thing. She grinned, a frank and engaging tomboy grin that woke her weathered features to liveliness.

'Come along to dinner,' she commanded. 'Leave the men to find their own way. I want to get to know you before they surround you and take up all your time. And they will! This is a house full of spoilt menfolk, make no mistake!' She tucked Marise's arm beneath her elbow and led her through another set of double doors into the immense dining room, which was lit by a cut-glass chandelier and hung with portraits so old the subjects seemed to be veiled in dark fog.

Hannibal's booming laugh followed them

into the dining room, where everyone took a place as he or she chose. Lina put Marise beside her and kept her busy answering questions. Ben, on her left, seemed both hungry and happy, ragging his brother and his father, teasing Lina and his wife.

Marise, watching him from time to time, was reassured. He had, indeed, regained his health at last. She followed him into the parlor, once dinner was over, and felt full and content as she accepted a cup of coffee before the crackling logs in the marble fireplace.

When they were settled comfortably, Father Clarrington had turned his dark eyes toward her. His voice was quiet, but it carried well in the small circle of velvet-covered chairs. 'You cannot begin to know, Marise, what pleasure you have brought us tonight. It has been a very long while since we had so much laughter, so much cheerful conversation in this old house. I'm afraid we've let ourselves become rather grim over the years.'

His black gaze probed hers, seeming to hold some hidden message. 'Life has a habit of taking the starch out of us. Out of our ambitions, our good humor, even out of our small stock of virtues. Things happen that nobody can foresee or forestall. They're nobody's fault, they just happen.

'You do the best you can with them. Or sometimes you don't do your best but jump up and down and curse fate, but neither one seems to change things one iota. We've done a lot of both, in this house, but now the sad old place has a chance to wake up. We're glad you've come. We're happy for Ben and happy for ourselves.'

'Hear! Hear!' rumbled Hannibal. 'My thoughts exactly. I'd have brought home a little porcelain lady myself, if I'd realized how it would perk things up. I haven't seen Mother look so happy in years.

'And Hildy! You've given her cooking a new lease on life. She used to complain that we could eat sawdust and never know the difference, but tonight she outdid herself. She had cooked for this same old crew for so long she was bored, but now she has a new palate to tempt.

You'd better watch it, or she'll put more meat on your bones than you might want to acquire. I believe she thinks thin is sinful.'

Marise smiled at him. 'I love Hildy. She was so sweet, after we got here. She tried to be the entire family rolled into one because she felt so bad about the way things turned out. But I never have met Andy yet. Does he stay all that busy?'

Hannibal glanced aside at Ben. Ben looked over at his father, who made a wry face. 'Andy is the cross we bear in order to keep Hildy. He's a good enough fellow, of course, does what he's asked to do cheerfully enough, when he's able. But he drinks. Not just a bit or just at times, but constantly. If I ever saw him sober, I probably would think he was drunk.

'He does get things done, though not always the way we'd like. For heaven's sake, never give him any vital message or depend on him to carry out anything of real importance. He can't remember at the top of the steps why he started up at the bottom.'

Aunt Lina snorted. 'He's not as far

gone as he pretends to be,' she said. 'You will notice that Andy can tend to Andy's business very well indeed. Hildy used to beat him, back when she was younger and had more energy, and that would keep him straight for months at a time. But now she's given up on reforming him.' She laughed suddenly and blushed.

'Hildy's fond of the old villain, that's the long and short of it. And Clarrington House without Hildy is unthinkable. Losing her would be just like losing the roof or the walls.'

Everyone laughed, and Marise sank more deeply into the comfort of her chair before the blazing logs. The coffee was hot, the room was warm, and the company was a close circle composed of family. She had not admitted to herself how she missed her own kin, and now she had another family who seemed to like and to welcome her.

She glanced at Ben, who leaned back in a wing chair, his legs stretched toward the fire. 'It's good to be home. I dreaded coming back for a long time, and business made sure that there wasn't time to. I hated to see Mother so ill, and I don't particularly like Edenson, though I know she's good to Mother. The old place has been . . . gloomy . . . for a long, long time. But that was my fault as much as anybody's, and now I feel I could spend the rest of my life here without any problem.

'Hanni, if you still want me to take over the logging interests, I'll be glad to. I never liked the work I did for that timber company up north. I think they're short-sighted in their management of resources, and I'd like a chance to take hold of our timber lands to see if my theories hold water. Do you think you can trust me with them?'

Hannibal was grinning widely, gripping his cup so tightly that Marise expected to see the thin china shatter. Father Clarrington was beaming as he swallowed audibly and gazed into the fire. 'Ben, it's what we've been waiting for since you got your forestry degree. We need your input and ideas, and we've just been waiting until you got ready. You were the one who left, remember?'

Ben and Hannibal reached across the

space between their chairs and grasped hands. 'The family firm,' Hannibal said. 'The Clarrington family firm. We've waited a long time, Ben.

'Father will be Chairman of the Board. I'll be the lawyer and investment expert. You're the forestry specialist. Only the farm is left without someone taking a real interest in it.' He cocked a slantwise gaze at Marise.

She shivered with excitement. 'I am a new and untried member of the family,' she said. 'But I'd love to manage that farm. I miss farming terribly, and I was truly a sound agriculturist. My father taught me all he knew, and he had learned from his father and so on for generations.

'We'd farmed right there on that same bit of ground since 1790. If one woman could have done the work of three strong people, I'd still be farming it. I had great plans and a lot of new things I wanted to try.'

'Then it will be a four-member firm,' Father Clarrington said. 'Welcome to Clarrington Enterprises, my dear. May we all work together happily for years to come.' His pale face was tinted by the flames to a healthy glow, and the lines had smoothed away for the moment. For an instant she saw his great likeness to Ben.

She reached impulsively to take his hand. 'I'm so happy!' she said.

Hannibal glanced at her sharply, his black eyes wary. 'Touch wood!' he said. 'It's dangerous to be too happy, and to know you are. We found that out a very long time ago.'

Not until long afterward had Marise understood what he meant.

*   *   *

Marise had no need of many clothes nowadays, but she still used the small sewing room on the first floor from time to time. Vigorous housework results in ripped seams and pulls or tears in shirt tails, no matter how careful you are.

This was one room she never locked. Seldom did she allow herself to think about what had happened there, though once in a while, as she turned the knob, she could hear Aunt Lina's gruff voice . . .

* * *

'Who is it?' asked Aunt Lina, in answer to Marise's knock.

'Only I, Auntie. I need to snip a loose thread in my hem.'

'Then come in, dear, and close the door. I've been wanting a word with you in private for a while. Come take that little chair by the window, and we'll kill two birds with the same stone. Where's the thread you need trimmed?' She took her small gold scissors and snipped off the offending ravel.

The sewing room was square with windows on adjacent walls, both looking out into the rose garden. A light snow, unusual this far south, had layered the shrubs and bare rose vines and the edging of lawn with crisp white.

Marise looked out at the scene, filled with pleasure. The snow light lit the room almost blindingly.

She glanced away from the window to

find Aunt Lina watching her, head cocked to one side, eyes speculative behind her rimless glasses. The older woman set down the sock she was mending and turned her low chair to face Marise's.

'Do you want children?' she asked. The question was so sudden and unexpected that Marise was startled. But Lina was sober to the point of grimness, and the younger woman felt a stab of concern.

'Why . . . we haven't discussed it yet, Aunt Lina. We married in quite a hurry, and there wasn't time to talk over a lot of things that people usually come to some agreement on beforehand. Ben was so ill . . . I asked his doctor, before he dismissed Ben, about that. I told him we were about to marry, and I needed to know if I should start birth control measures, but Dr. Field thought Ben's sickness, whatever it might be, would not be hereditary.' She thought back to that interview, trying to remember Field's exact words.

'He said it would be months before Ben would be fertile again, because of the array of drugs they tried on him. Some of the treatments leave traces in the system for a long time. But he didn't seem concerned at the prospect of Ben's marrying and possibly having a family, when the time comes.' She grinned cheerfully. 'And my family is about as healthy as you can get, which farmers tend to be.'

Lina shook her head. 'You don't quite understand, child. It isn't your heredity I'm concerned with . . . but it relieves me to know that it will be a while before you have to worry about it, anyway. There are things you don't know about this family.' She picked up the sock and bit off a thread with the same crisp motion Marise recalled, dimly, her own mother using.

Lina threaded her needle, picked up another sock, and took three tiny stitches, one on top of the other, to anchor her thread. For some odd reason she seemed to be delaying the beginning of this private talk as long as she could.

Marise rose and knelt beside the low chair, reaching to hold Lina's hands still. 'Aunt Lina, what are you trying to tell me?' She felt the chill of the long fingers between her own, and rubbed her hands together to warm them.

A tear dropped onto her fingers and Lina wiped her eyes with her sweater sleeve. She sniffed rather loudly and cleared her throat.

'Nobody likes to talk about bad things in their own families,' she said at last. 'I don't, and you wouldn't if there were anything really wrong in your heredity. But there's bad blood in our line. Not criminal. I wish it was that simple. It's *madness*.'

Marise felt a surge of surprise and shock. 'Auntie, are you certain? I never in my life met anyone more sane and sensible than you and your brother. Not to mention Ben and Hannibal; they're almost too brilliant for their own good.'

Lina rubbed her eyes, loosing Marise's hands to do so. That allowed her to avoid looking straight at the girl as she spoke. 'There have been afflicted children born, at least one to each generation for the past three.' She sounded hoarse, as if the words were difficult to speak.

'But not in Ben's generation!' Marise said. Ben's aunt did not contradict her.

34

'Emanuel and I swore not to marry,' Lina went on. 'I kept my vow, but when he met Elizabeth, he seemed to forget about that and all the other things we had taken into consideration.

'Perhaps . . . perhaps if I had met someone I loved, who truly loved me, I'd have done the same. I judge him harshly, I know, and that may be because I'm jealous of his family. But I've spent my life thinking about what might happen because my brother fell in love. I'm afraid. Afraid for you and Ben, if you decide to have a baby.'

Marise stared into Lina's pained eyes. She still didn't understand what drove Lina to this desperation, but she knew, whatever its cause and however valid her concern was, it was totally genuine.

That had been the end of their conversation. Marise puzzled over it for weeks, trying to see in any of the Clarringtons around her a hint of eccentricity or mental imbalance. She found nothing at all to disturb her. In fact, she had more cause to doubt her own sanity than that of any of the family.

That was because the house itself troubled her. She woke in the night, hearing odd sounds, the remnants of lost echoes or whispers or tappings. Once she left a book in the sitting room and went down, after going to bed, to retrieve it.

She still recalled standing in the dim-lit room, holding the book, listening to the scrabbling noise that seemed to come from the door onto the stair. It had been disturbing, though she told herself it was a mouse in the paneling. The old building was overrun with the creatures, and she had heard them in the space above her bedroom ceiling.

But this sounded as if someone was trying to open the door. Ben had put a bolt on the inside and cautioned her to use it always, if she was the last to come to bed. 'In our home?' she'd asked him, feeling incredulous. 'What could possibly harm us here?'

He'd looked tired and harassed, but he answered calmly enough: 'Call it a hangover from my illness. I just don't feel secure unless it's fastened. Do it for me, love. I have lived for so long, in so many odd places, and among such strange sorts of people that it has shaken my nerve. Do it for me.'

Of course she had, faithfully, and that night she had been glad of the strong bolt. The fumbling and scratching had sounded as if it were on the other side of the solid door. She kept insisting to herself that if it wasn't a mouse, it was a squirrel in the wall, and she knew that had to be true.

Yet after that night she felt obscurely nervous as she went about the house. She would have the sense of being watched in the oddest locations. Once, sitting in the kitchen before Hildy's beaming gaze, she had suddenly felt her back go cold, as if someone stared at it. When she made some reason to turn, there was no one there, and she had known that would be true.

'I'm getting notional,' she told herself sternly. 'There's nothing wrong with me, and there's nothing wrong with anyone else here. It's just living in a house that is so much bigger than I'm used to.'

She also began being nauseated, and

she attributed that to nerves. But, in a few weeks more, after Ben sent her to the doctor who had treated the family for half a generation, she learned the problem was not in her mind. Despite what Dr. Field had told her, she was pregnant.

The night after that was confirmed beyond doubt, when Ben came into her bedroom she met him with such a joyful face that he had known at once something exciting was happening. 'We're going to be parents!' she said, forgetting entirely the qualms Lina had tried to instill in her. She caught him by the elbows and whirled him around the room until they fell, laughing, onto the bed.

'There is going to be another Clarrington to brighten up this gloomy old house. I am so happy!'

He sat up then, very slowly and carefully. Taking her shoulders into his hands, he looked at her solemnly. His eyes held happiness, affection . . . and a trace of fear. That was natural, she thought. He never had been a father before.

'I'm so happy, Doll,' he said. 'But promise me something. Tell Aunt Lina before you tell anyone else. Tell her in private. She . . . has a special interest. And my parents won't be upset by that.'

'I know she'll be interested,' Marise said, remembering that odd conversation earlier. 'She talked with me once, for a while. I never did quite understand what she was getting at. I'll go to her tomorrow and tell her.'

Ben kissed her then, very tenderly, but that night he cried out in his sleep as he had not done for months. She patted him quiet without waking him, there in the darkness, wondering what it could be that he feared so terribly.

The next morning she tapped once again on the sewing room door, to hear Aunt Lina's deep voice bid her to enter. Lina looked up at her over the tops of her glasses, her jade green eyes full of laughter at some nonsense she was listening to on the radio at her elbow. The laughter faded as she looked more closely at her visitor.

Marise sat in the low chair again. It was very like that other day, she thought, as she reached to take the woman's hand. 'Auntie, I've come to tell you something wonderful. Something Ben thinks you should know before anyone else in the family.

'The doctor was wrong. Ben wasn't sterile at all. We're going to have a baby.'

As Marise watched in horror, Lina's face turned gray, literally gray, as if the accumulated essence of old age and death washed across it, leaving nothing but devastation behind. The big hand struggled free of her own and grasped the arm of the chair as if holding to some dream of security.

'What is wrong?' Marise had cried, going to her knees beside the sewing chair. 'Aunt Lina, are you ill?'

'Pay it no mind. I have . . . little spells, now and again. When I get excited.' Lina drew a long breath, held it for a moment, and let it out again. She straightened in the chair and managed a weak smile.

'Never think, child, about that nonsense I told you before. We all take risks constantly, all through our lives. You have a greater chance of having a sound child than an unsound one, and I'm an old fool.

'Just because I wasted my life and my youth doesn't mean that everybody else has to do it too. Take my hand and help me up. We have to go down and tell Emanuel and Elizabeth the news, or they'll never forgive us.'

They had gone together, through this very door. Marise touched it, and it opened, revealing the now dim interior. The chair in which Aunt Lina had stitched so many miles of seams and darns and mends stood empty, of course, except for memories.

This older Marise sighed. Even pain grows dim, in time.

3

Marise hated going into the big kitchen almost more than any other room in the house. Hildy's bright yellow curtains still hung at the windows, kept washed and starched crisp by Marise's hands. The huge cook stove and the Formica-topped work-table cried out, even now, for Hildy's ample shape, her capable hands, her strange little chicken-peep of a voice.

Marise had not realized until too late that Hildy, more even than Father Clarrington, was the heart of Clarrington House. The furnace itself had no more to do with keeping the place warm and alive than the big cook had done.

Marise sighed as she put the kettle onto a burner, took bread from the plastic breadbox, and brought little dabs of this and that from the great refrigerator. The shelves looked cavernous, interrupted only by her piddling bits of food.

Her supply of perishables was getting

low, even considering how little she ate. She reached up to make a notation on the pad beside the telephone. It was time, once more, to call the Trustees and have their man bring what she needed.

Turning, she poured hot water into the warmed teapot and set her scrappy meal on the table. She ate at the small one where Hildy had served coffee or tea or cookies to anyone who came, no matter how unusual the hour. The cook had been sitting here . . .

*   *   *

Hildy smacked biscuit dough with a plump fist, turning and pummeling it until a light mist of flour rose into the air. The rich smell of the roast in the oven was already making Marise's mouth water; she nibbled at a whole-grain wafer Hildy had prescribed for her, along with milk, every day.

Something made Marise feel mischievous. She had never been particularly inclined in that direction before her pregnancy, but it seemed to have brought

43

out the devilment in her nature.

'Hildy,' she asked innocently, 'when are you going to show me the whole of the third floor? I know Aunt Lina's room well, and we're working on the old nursery and schoolroom, getting them ready for future use. But all the rooms around the bend at the other end of the corridor are ones I've never seen.'

This was not quite the innocent question it seemed, for Marise had been noticing that any mention of the rear part of the third floor made every one of the Clarrington family uneasy.

It didn't really bother her. She had been too busy with making her own suite into a comfortable nest, as well as working on the nursery, to bother with any more of this endless house and its seemingly uncountable rooms.

Hildy's hands jerked, and she turned to look at Marise. Her new hearing aid was helping, but she still didn't trust her ears.

'You said?' she asked.

'I asked about the third floor. I've never seen even half of it.'

'Plenty time for that later,' Hildy said,

giving the dough a solid thump. 'You take one look at the musty old rooms back there, you go crazy to clean, to fix nice. No way you can do that now.

'I'd be shamed to let you see how we let the old place go, since I get old and achy.' The big hands flipped the dough, smoothed it expertly, flattened it on the special board in a puff of flour dust, and began patting it flat. No rolling pin did the job to suit Hildy.

Her pale golden hair wisped around her face in strands that had escaped from her hairnet. Her pale eyes did not rise to meet Marise's questioning gaze.

'It's really odd,' Marise mused. 'Nobody will take me up there. Even Ben, when he's home at all, won't even bother to do it. And there's so much room back there I was thinking we might set up an indoor gym or something like that, when the baby gets old enough to need a place to play on rainy days. Don't you think that would be nice for him?'

'Nice, yes, but who would do it? Everyone very busy, including you. That farm take much of your time, and I don't see you turn it loose, even after the baby come.'

Marise sighed. 'I suppose you're right. I seem to have too much energy right now, even with all the things I'm doing. And I only go out to the farm two or three times a week, since the doctor warned me to take it easier. I seem mostly to sit and fidget. Maybe I should just go up and explore by myself.'

'No!' Hildy's voice was thin shrill, almost terrified. 'Promise me you not do that, Marri. This . . . this is very old house, not all in good repair. There is soft floor, loose woodwork back there. Also spiders, very many, and rats. Even some black widow spiders I have seen. You do not need spider bite, with the baby so near. Promise!'

Marise realized that she was even paler than her usual Scandinavian fairness would warrant. Her tone verged on the frantic.

Filled with remorse, she reassured Hildy at once. 'Why, of course. I promise, Hildy. I don't want to give you any more worry, on top of all the work you have to do. I hate having Ben away so much. I suppose that's the real reason why I'm so restless.'

The fair face was flushed again from the heat of the stove and her own exertions. Hildy beamed at her with approval. 'Exactly so. You lonely for Ben, since he is so busy in woods. There is not so much for you to do around the house, too.

'Maybe you go walk in the garden? Or along street? Walk is good exercise and not too hard for you.'

'I just might do that.' Marise rose and set her cup and plate in the sink. 'It's nice and windy. That will keep it from being too hot, if I stay in the shade. Good idea, Hildy.' She smiled and left the kitchen, leaving the door open to the breeze that pulled through the hall.

She had almost reached the front door when Hildy called after her. She turned, struck by the odd note in the old woman's voice.

'Marri, we all love you. You make Ben happy. You make him well, when he might die. You make Hanni smile, Mr. Clarrington laugh, the Mrs. feel better. We do not want anything to happen. We want baby to come, fine and healthy, no trouble.

'Maybe we try too hard to keep you safe, yes? But it is because you bring life to a house that has been dead for a very long time. This is not a good house. Not always.

'Some very bad things happen up there on the third floor. They make us all unhappy, even now, and afraid too. Even so much later, we are still afraid. Please, Marri, do not go back along the corridor on the third floor?' Her voice was pleading.

Marise laughed and went back through the open door to take the floury hand held out to her. 'Why, Hildy, I promised. Of course I won't go there. But what *did* happen up there? My imagination will make up all sorts of horror stories until I know the truth.'

Hildy chose her words with such care that her accent all but disappeared. 'It is not my place to speak of my employers' troubles. We have been together for very many years, but still I am their servant. I have no right to tell you things that Mr.

Clarrington may not want you to know, so soon.

'Perhaps you have not seen that hesitation in him. I know how it is when you are young. You think always about making a good impression on others. They also, you might see, want for you to like them.'

Marise squeezed the big hand. 'I will ask him, then. You are quite right, Hildy. I shouldn't have tried to worm information out of you.' She hugged the plump figure for an instant, feeling the constant warmth and solidity of the woman.

'And don't try to fool me that you're a servant. You're one of the family, if any of us are. We all come to you when we're depressed or restless or just hungry! Don't sell yourself short!'

Hildy's high, tinkling laugh had followed her through the corridor and out the front door.

★ ★ ★

Now the bright curtains still made the room look as if sun shone outside, even

49

though the late fall day had turned gray beyond the windows. Marise thought of her joyous young self, walking through this room, the corridors, all the other rooms in this big pile of a house.

She had been unknowing, hopeful for the future. She had trusted fate to guide her correctly.

She chinked her dirty dishes together into the dishwasher, measured detergent, turned on the switch. Of the eight people, family and servants and child, who had lived here together, only she remained.

Now she dared not set her foot outside the front door. Even though she was healthy, still in early middle age, she did not trust fate, or the world, or (and this she found it difficult to admit to herself) her own reactions and abilities. The world might not be dangerous to her, but she was terribly, frighteningly uncertain whether she might not be dangerous to it.

She sighed heavily and moved into the corridor, closing the door upon the bright room. Once more the grateful shadows sheltered her.

Marise dialed and listened to the ring at the office end of the line. One . . . two . . . three . . . four . . . Mrs. Fisk was not her usual prompt self, taking all the calls to see what was going on.

'Clarrington Enterprises. Mrs. Fisk.' The voice was sharper than usual.

'This is Marise Clarrington, Mrs. Fisk. Is Evan in? I need to speak with him.'

'He's not in this morning, Mrs. Clarrington. I am taking his clients today. He went to Washington to lobby for the timber bill. May I help you? He left word it was time for your monthly call.' There was an avid quality to that voice, and Marise had a sudden realization that Fisk had some unnatural interest in her affairs. But what couldn't be cured must be endured.

'Thank you, Mrs. Fisk. If you don't mind, I need to have my usual order of groceries delivered. I called my order to the super-market, and the manager will have them ready tomorrow at noon. If your young man will pick them up and bring them out, I will appreciate it. I have just mailed the instructions for the fall plantings at the farm. Evan should have those tomorrow. I also need to see the balance sheets on the entire operation, farm, timber, securities, and the Trust as well, as soon as he has time to prepare them.' She heard a sharp intake of breath from Fisk.

'If he would like, he might bring those by. If he hasn't the time, he might mail them. Either is fine.'

Gertrude Fisk's voice came again. 'Of course, Mrs. Clarrington. Is there anything else? I'd be glad to oblige.'

Marise almost laughed aloud. 'No, but thank you. Some month you might like to bring the papers for me to sign yourself, and we can meet.' She spoke casually, trying to sound cordial.

But she was left with an odd sense of foreboding. There was more to Mrs. Fisk than had heretofore met her eye.

★ ★ ★

Only twice a year did Marise enter the study that had belonged to Emanuel Clarrington. Even now, it breathed with his presence, the scent of his pipe tobacco lingering still. It had been ten years since he left it for the last time, but she felt him in the room with an intensity that was almost painful.

The big mahogany desk still held his leather-trimmed blotter, the penholder, the open file where his most pressing correspondence had been kept. She had left the volume of *King Lear* open on the corner of his desk, as he had left it. She dusted under it on her twice-yearly visits and then returned it carefully, still open to the page on which Lear's madness was made so plain.

That was probably a sign of her own lack of mental balance, she often thought. Such minute attention to preserving the last remnants of the past should not be possible to a healthy mind.

She still remembered the many long talks she had shared here with the man who became a second father to her. His rich voice seasoned the very covers of the law and reference volumes that lined the bookcases. She had never expected her father-in-law to become so much a part of her life.

Emanuel Clarrington had been her mentor. He had led her into philosophical fields that she had never considered before, and he had coached her as she tackled endeavors she had never thought she would have the chance to try. She measured her physical adulthood from her marriage to Ben. Her intellectual maturity stemmed from her father-in-law.

He had been strong yet gentle. As she had promised Hildy she would do, she had come to him with her questions about that upstairs room. He had gone even paler than usual when she asked about it.

'Sit down, Marise,' he had said softly. 'Did you close the door? Yes, I see you did. Would you like a sherry?'

'This early? Not quite, Father Clarrington!' She remembered laughing at his expression.

Then she sobered as he replied, 'Well, I would. I have to have something to brace me up when I think about . . . certain things.' He poured a generous slosh from the cut glass decanter, and she saw that his hand was unsteady. Then, holding the delicate glass, he took his seat behind the big desk, as if seeking refuge.

Marise felt guilty for troubling him with her intrusive question.

'Really, Father, if it distresses you I can live without knowing. I'm getting to be fanciful, partly because of the baby, I suspect. Don't feel awkward about telling me that there are some things I don't need to know. I didn't really realize what I was asking of you.'

'No.' His voice was sad. 'But why should you be expected to? You are, for better or worse, one of us now. It is your right to know, and we should have told you about this painful truth at once. But I hated to do anything to upset the balance of things.

'Ben seemed so happy and relaxed that I hesitated to do or say anything to worry you. It might have affected him. We're not a demonstrative family, Marise. But we do care very deeply for each other.'

'There simply cannot be that big a skeleton in the family closet,' she said, keeping her tone light. 'I can't think of anything that would make me leave

Clarrington House.'

'You don't know, child. You don't know,' he said. His thin hand shook again as he lifted the glass to his lips. Then he said, 'You can't know until I tell you, and I'm finding it hard to begin.'

Again he lifted the glass, draining it as if for courage. When he set it down, he clasped his fingers together and began, 'You must allow me to go back a bit in time, for our problems as a family began in England.

'Our people were very well to do, baronets in the eighteenth and early nineteenth centuries. Like most of their peers, they laid a lot of emphasis on material wealth — land, houses, horses, money. They held onto those things with an energy that deserved a worthier focus. For three generations, cousins married cousins, so the estate might grow to add adjacent holdings.

'You, being a nurse, must know that inbreeding is a matter deserving of caution. Strong genes can reinforce each other and make for strong people, but defective ones can also double up. And there was a flawed gene in our line. It didn't show up for quite a long time. It seemed for a while that the Clarringtons were going to get away with their game of genetic roulette.

'They had many children, bright, forceful, aggressive young men and women who were ornaments to the breed. Some went into the army and won medals. Some went into Parliament and made several significant changes for the betterment of the common people. My ancestors began to feel they were a favored race, invincible and invulnerable.'

She rose and filled his glass from the decanter and he nodded absently, locked into that sad old history. He sipped again, and the wine seemed to bring a bit of color back into his thin cheeks. 'They were wrong, of course. In the third generation, all hell broke loose.

'Of six children in that generation, four were eccentric to the point of madness. One was normal. One was quite dangerously insane. According to the tradition brought to us by our own ancestor, the one seemingly normal child in that brood, the sixth child, managed at a very early age to murder two of the four children who were merely odd and unusual. All were older than she.'

'She?' Marise felt horrified fascination as the tale unfolded.

'She. A lovely little girl with the face of an angel, my father's grandfather used to say. But she had the soul of an imp from hell. Her agonized parents refused to put her in Bedlam, for they couldn't bear to send her into such squalid and terrible conditions.

'At times she could be so adorable they could never quite bring themselves to believe her guilty of the horrible incident that took the lives of her two brothers. It had to be some sort of accident, they kept insisting.' He sighed and looked down at his blotter, then up at Marise.

'My ancestor, fearful of what might happen, gave up his inheritance and came to the New World. That was just as well for the continuance of the line, for two years after he left, Clarrington Hall burned to the ground with everyone in the family, including servants, trapped inside. Nobody had any theories as to how the conflagration happened or why the outer doors were all stuck fast, but he had his own dreadful suspicions.'

Marise shivered but managed to keep herself from looking appalled. 'But that's several generations in the past, Father. Surely there has been enough mixture of the genes by now to eliminate any taint there might have been.'

'You would think so,' he agreed. 'But you would not be correct. My own father had a twin brother. He was brilliant, a musician and a mathematician in the exciting combination that happens from time to time.

'When he was ten he made his debut at Carnegie Hall. The Juilliard accepted him as a student instructor when he was twenty. When he was twenty-two, the arson squad in New York found that he had been setting fires in the tenement districts in the city on the nights when he wasn't otherwise occupied with music.'

That was too close for comfort, but Marise still managed to control her reactions. 'What happened to him? Was he sent into a mental home?'

'He killed himself before his sanity could be examined,' said Emanuel. His fingers pressed against the blotter so hard that even the nails had turned white.

'Still, this was a couple of generations back. It's hardly an immediate cause for alarm. And how does that connect with the third floor of this house?' she asked.

'One of those rooms was his. He equipped it himself, with bars over the windows, for he was terrified of intruders, prowlers, burglars. His door was studded with locks, and he killed himself there. His family had to shatter the door to get to him. Too late, of course.'

She studied his face, now drawn and dreadfully weary. 'There's something else. I can see it in your eyes.'

He drew a deep breath. 'Yes, and that is the worst of all. I had a sister, Clara. I always thought it a terrible name, Clara Clarrington. But she was lovely, with long brown hair, the black Clarrington eyes. She was quick, talented, impish. I adored her.'

He turned to stare out of the window beside his desk, into the sunlight angled across the garden, his face lined with pain.

'Looking back, it seems she grew up in constant sunlight. I always see her, when I remember, dancing in the garden, round and round the rockery with the sundial in the middle. Round and round and round.

'I went to join her, and when I took her hands to swing her around, as she loved for me to do, I found that she had pounded the head of one of my pups with a rock and laid the little smashed body on the sundial. She was dancing around her victim. Her sacrifice.'

He looked down again as if avoiding that dreadful sunlight outside. 'People lie to themselves, you know. I told myself this was something children often do. Abuse of animals is by no means rare in the very young. They grow out of it, I insisted to myself.

'But I always had a niggling doubt. I remembered those old tales my grandfather told about his family, and they made me nervous.

'Until then I did not properly appreciate my other sister, Angelina. Lina. She was not pretty. Her talents were practical, unspectacular ones. She gardened productively. She could make a room glow with beauty and comfort, and she could make anyone talking with her feel as if he were brilliant, witty, sophisticated.

'She still does that. And she was the only one I told about the incident with the pup. We promised each other we would never marry and carry on the taint we felt was living inside our little sister. We watched her closely. Indeed, we were so careful of her that she grew into her mid-teens without another problem coming to light.

'We conveniently ignored the fact that pets in our neighborhood tended to disappear frequently. One of the servants died, but we assured ourselves it was of natural causes. The boy who helped the gardener became very ill, and to this day I have no idea whether that was natural or not, but he died in the little cottage that used to stand beside the coach house. The incident frightened us, rightly or wrongly.'

Softly, Marise asked, 'You never told your parents?'

He shook his white head. 'You see, we couldn't actually prove anything. Not even that she had been the one who killed my puppy, all those years ago. We just felt in our blood and bones that the family defect had come down in Clara.

'We forgot we must grow up and go away to live lives of our own. She was still very young when Lina went away to school. I was sent to Harvard Law School. We left her here with our parents and the servants and her governess.'

'So she wasn't sent away to school.'

'No. We persuaded Father and Mother it was better to have her taught at home because she was too brilliant to waste time with standard teaching methods. And that was true. She was incredibly apt at everything, music, maths, writing, dancing.

'I managed to hint to Father that it would be wise to watch her closely, but he misunderstood. I realized that too late. He thought I was an over-fond brother, jealous of possible suitors.' He almost managed a smile.

'And her room, too, was on the third

floor?' Marise asked.

'Eventually, once it was obvious that she was too dangerous to allow her to mix with other people. By the time my father realized it, by the time I was mature enough to tell him frankly what I feared, a neighbor's child had died. Beaten to death with a rock.'

'Not near the sundial!' Marise gasped.

'No, in the garden of the house next door, where the vacant lot is now. He lived in the house beyond that, and children often played in the garden, for the old couple who lived there loved to have youngsters around them. I knew at once it had been no chance intruder who killed him. Clara had mentioned him often, before I left for college.

'That was when I flew home and confronted Father with everything I knew and feared and suspected. By then, he had some fears of his own, but it took both of us to convince Mother that Clara had to be confined.'

Marise sat up straight, understanding at once. 'In your uncle's room, of course. It was already barred, and the door wouldn't be hard to replace, even more strongly than it was at first. Oh, my dear man! What a tragedy for you and your family!'

He nodded. 'Much worse than a burden. Mother never accepted the fact that her youngest and most beautiful child was a monster. Not until entirely too late did she believe her lovely Clara was dangerously demented. We learned she used to visit her secretly, though Father warned her never to go into the room without someone else there.

'Mother was small, frail, much like you. Clara was tall and slender and very strong. The strength of madness? I've often wondered.' He stood abruptly and fetched the decanter again to refill his glass.

'You mean . . . she killed her own mother?' Marise's whisper was filled with horror.

'It wasn't that neat and tidy,' he said, his tone bitter. 'She always behaved well when Mother came to see her. She made Mother believe we accused her unjustly and confined her for some strange, sick reason of our own. She convinced Mother that she was an innocent, imprisoned without cause, and Mother bought it.

'She wanted to believe that, and she connived with Clara to get her out of the house with money enough to take her to our aunt in Charlottesville, where she could take refuge. She went up one night, when Father was asleep, with cash, a traveling bag all packed, and a bus ticket to Charlottesville. She intended to save this persecuted daughter.' He shuddered.

'I have envisioned that night many times, when I couldn't sleep. I know Clara must have met her with smiles and kisses. But Father must have waked for some unknown reason. Perhaps his intuition was working overtime, but however it was he went upstairs to make certain things were secure. He found Clara standing over Mother's body, still holding onto the stocking with which she had strangled her.

'Father was big, like Hannibal, not just tall but bulky and tough and strong. He told me she came at him like a she-bear. He broke her neck with one chop. Then he called the police chief, who was his old friend and schoolmate. He told him everything and offered to go to jail right then if Nate Rivers thought it was right.

'Nate didn't. He got hold of the District Attorney and he and the police chief got together downstairs and fixed up an 'accident.' It's mighty convenient to have pots of old money and an influential family background. There were friends in the right places to cover up a family scandal.

'Sometimes I think it's entirely too easy. If it had all come out then, maybe we wouldn't be haunted by those old deaths even up to the present. Madness and murder, that's our skeleton. It's a big one, don't you think?' He looked intently at Marise.

She deliberately relaxed the tension in her neck and arms and back. She thought she must have been holding her breath.

'I see. No wonder you hate the thought of that room up there. Logical or not, those psychological ghosts are haunting the whole area, and I can see why Aunt Lina warned me about having children, too. But surely we're far enough away by now so it's not such a threat?' She asked the question almost pleadingly.

'I devoutly hope so,' he said. He turned the glass in his fine fingers. 'The burden of such a heritage can be devastating, and I know it better than most. Lina has never understood how I could forget that and marry Elizabeth. But I need not tell you falling in love erases a lot of things from your mind.

'I wanted Elizabeth, needed her more than air or water or even life. Our sons are the finest men I know, even if having Ben did mean a lifetime of invalidism for my wife. We didn't know until Ben that the strain on her heart was going to be so drastic. But I am not sure that, even knowing what we know now, we would not make the same choices again.'

Marise rose and put her hand on his shoulder, patting it softly. 'I cannot be sorry you had Ben,' she said. 'Or Hannibal, either. He's like one of my own brothers. I was an orphan when I met Ben, and you have given me a family to love. We'll think positively. Ben's baby and mine can't be anything but sound and strong, now can he?'

He had patted her hand then, but his eyes did not meet hers. 'Surely your child must be. So much love and so many good wishes are going to accompany him into the world. We hoped to spare you the worry of this old tragedy. We felt it wouldn't be good for you to have to deal with it at this point.

'We never meant to exclude you from family secrets or to make you feel like an outsider. Concern, not secretiveness, kept you from the third floor rooms,' he said, but she could see his fingers gripping the glass still.

'Clara's room has not been unlocked since the men carried away her body and Mother's. Not cleaned, not straightened.'

But not until much later did Marise know that of all the strange things he had told her, only that had been a lie.

* ★ ★

Marise still used the conservatory, although a number of the exotic plants had died in the past ten years. Of old age, she was sure, for she had tended them faithfully as long as they lasted.

Now she planted spinach and tomatoes and cucumbers in the planters, and harvested her own salad greens and many other vegetables. She felt this might be the only normal and healthy thing she did now. The fresh scents soothed her wounded spirit, and the feel of the soil between her fingers was comforting.

The wide French doors of the dining room opened onto the glassed enclosure, and she always drew a deep breath when she stepped through. A number of ornamental vines and a few long-lived shrubs in huge pots still lived to fill the air with their fragrance. This had been one of Mother Clarrington's favorite haunts, and Edenson used to bring her there to sit, when she felt able to be up for a while.

Then there had been banks of tropical plants in long clay planters, and orchids hanging from the two palms that still rattled stiff fronds at either end of the room. The damp fragrance seemed to enliven the invalid, and she had seemed more nearly normal there than anyplace.

She had called Marise to her side one day, shortly before the baby was due. 'Come and sit beside me and let me hold your hand,' she'd said. 'I know you must be nervous. I was terrified before Hannibal was born. But perhaps your generation has lost the fears mine was heir to. The old wives' tales I was told would have frightened an Amazon, and I was certainly not a bold woman.'

Marise perched on a stool beside the chair. 'Remember that I'm a nurse,' she said. 'I've helped to deliver many babies, and I have even delivered them on my own, in a pinch. Nobody can tell me anything I haven't seen with my own eyes.

'I am exercising, to make the birth easier and Ben and I are going to Lamaze classes. I hope to do this naturally, without anesthesia because it's better for the baby. But Dr. Pell seems concerned with the width of my pelvis, so I'm not going to be hardheaded about it, for I trust his judgment.'

'Good. That is always best, and we have trusted Dr. Pell for many years. I don't know whether to hope for a boy or a girl.

I love little boys, but a girl would be lovely. My little girl . . . ' — she caught her lip between her teeth and looked alarmed.

'But you had only the two boys, I thought,' Marise said.

Mrs. Clarrington looked down at her hands. 'My little girl . . . died. I never really had her at all. I was so ill at the time that no matter what happened, I wouldn't have been able to take care of her, and I never got any better. Not really.'

She caught her breath sharply. 'You cannot know, my dear, how many prayers I say for you and Ben. For your health and happiness and the child's. We've been such a sad family for so long, I'm afraid the habit of fearing the worst is ingrained in us. You are good for us. I just hope we're not bad for you.'

Marise tapped her arm playfully. 'That's morbid! Think happy thoughts, Mother Clarrington. That's what I am doing, and Ben is helping, when he's at home. He seems so excited about the baby, but he's a bit apprehensive too. After what Father Clarrington told me about the family heredity, I suppose that's natural.'

The woman's face turned pale. She gripped Marise's fingers and gasped, 'Call Edenson. I must go up to bed. Happy thoughts . . . they did me no good at all. Dear, do call Edenson!'

The nurse had wheeled her away, her head leaning back against the tall back of the chair, her hands too limp to work the controls. All the strength seemed to have run out of her like water through a sieve. One pale hand moved feebly in farewell, as they passed through the French doors.

Something about that conversation left Marise unsettled and uneasy. There never had been any mention of another child in Ben's generation. Surely her husband would have told her, if there had been.

She knew Mrs. Clarrington had been terribly ill after Ben's birth and never could have another child, so this unnamed daughter would have to have come between Hannibal and Ben. But she said she had been ill since that birth, which meant she should not have had Ben at all. It was strange.

The baby had chosen that time to kick strenuously. She rose from the stool to give it more room for its efforts, and standing there, surrounded by the sweet humid air, she had been thinking of nothing in particular. A feeling of dim foreboding had been the worst of her sensations, when a sound came to her ears.

It was a soft, high voice, singing. A childish song quavered in the air, perhaps a nursery rhyme. And it came from nearby, someplace overhead, though she knew that was impossible. Only the sky rose over the conservatory. And, of course, the rooms on the third floor.

★　★　★

Marise sank onto her heels and thrust her trowel into the dirt. Patting soil around the roots of a newly transplanted aloe vera, she thought of that childish voice. She could almost hear its echo, all these years afterward.

She shuddered, stood, and left the room, closing the French doors firmly behind her.

4

If Marise avoided the study as much as possible, the library was the room she dreaded with all her being. Though she loved to read and went often to browse along the packed shelves, she always entered with a cold shudder along her spine.

It was here she had found Hannibal. That memory would never leave her.

Little Ben was about five, she remembered, and he had been with her. They were searching out easy reading books left from his father's and uncle's childhoods. Already, the child was reading well for one so young and so busy with projects of his own.

She still felt his square little paw, warm in her hand, as she opened the wide door and snapped on the lights. Outside it was a dismal October day, just right for reading together.

The sturdy little figure ran ahead into the room and turned toward the low shelf in the corner where his own particular books were kept. She wandered along the shelves, taking down volumes at random and flipping through their pages before replacing them.

She had been in the mood for a good mystery. Nothing as ladylike as Agatha Christie. Nor yet the aggressive *macho* of Mike Hammer. She wanted something refined and yet shivery. Ngaio Marsh? Yes, that was the ticket.

She moved over to the long library table and bent to pull out one of the red velvet chairs that sat solemnly about it. When she glanced over the table, her eyes looked directly down into Hannibal's. He lay on his back between the table and the wall of shelves behind it.

No one knew death better than she. A spasm of nausea shook her as she stared into those unseeing eyes. Hannibal, big and tough and endearing, was lying dead on the library carpet, his face drawn into a rictus of pain. His hands were clamped tightly over his heart.

Marise needed to scream or to cry, but she did neither of those things. With iron control, she placed her book on the table, carefully squaring its edge with that of the wood. She pushed the chair back into place, concealing Hannibal's feet beneath the table.

'Have you found a book yet?' she called to Benjie. 'Two,' he said with pride. 'I think I can read these two.' He rose from his crouch before the shelves, clutching the books to his chest. He looked entirely too much like Hannibal! She choked down tears and smiled at her son. His black eyes sparkled back at her.

She kept her control, though later she had wondered how she managed. 'Then let's go. You can take your books upstairs to the schoolroom by yourself, can't you? I need to speak to Grandpa a minute.'

He looked surprised and hurt, for they had planned to read together. 'Go by the kitchen and tell Hildy I said it's all right to give you two cookies. Just two, then upstairs. All right?'

'All right,' he answered, with his usual good cheer. 'Two cookies? Choc chip?'

'Chocolate chip,' she agreed, controlling

her need to hurry him away from that dreadful room.

When he had trotted away down the hall she drew a deep breath and stilled the shaking of her hands. She tapped at the study door, feeling a cold lump of despair in her stomach.

Emanuel had been seated at his desk, the ledgers spread out in orderly disarray about him. He looked up with an absent expression. 'Oh, come in. Did you need something?'

He looked at her more closely, then rose and came around the desk. 'Marise, what on earth is wrong?'

She leaned against the door. 'I don't know how to tell you this,' she choked. 'Hannibal . . . ' but a small voice said from the doorway, 'I go up now, Mama?'

She turned and managed another strained smile. 'You go up now, sweetheart. I may be a while coming. You read to yourself until I come, all right?'

When his small feet thumped away up the stair, she felt the blood drain away behind her eyes. Without speaking, she flopped into a chair and put her head between her knees.

When the dizziness faded, she looked up to find Father Clarrington kneeling beside her. 'Marise, what is it?'

'Hannibal's dead,' she said without preamble. 'In the library, behind the long table. He . . . looks as if he had a heart attack. His hands are tight against his chest. Call Ben, Father. Or whoever. I think I'm going to be sick, and that's disgraceful for someone who has seen as much death as I have.'

But she didn't get sick. Never in her life had she collapsed in an emergency, and that relief was denied her now. She waited in the study, watching her father-in-law call the forest management office.

'Clarrington here,' he said. 'Put out a call for Ben, will you, Mark? He should be out somewhere in the pine plantation. Send someone out after him, if you need to. There's . . . been a death in the family.'

A quick question squawked from the phone. 'No, not his mother. Don't let it get out yet, but Hannibal just died. Yes, a terrible shock.'

He listened for a moment and said,

'Thank you, Mark. Yes. We will. God bless you too.' He set the phone in its cradle and wiped tears from his eyes.

Again he dialed. 'Angus? Well, is he there at all? Where? Can you give me that number? Thank you, Evie.'

His fingers trembled on the dial. The buzz of the phone ringing was audible, even to Marise. She heard the click as the receiver was lifted.

'Mrs. Anderson? This is Emanuel Clarrington. Is Sheriff Lederer there? Yes, I'll hold. I understand. I'll wait.'

He covered the mouthpiece with one hand and said, 'Angus is out at Anderson's, looking into something about a stolen tractor. She's getting him.'

Marise waited, numb and sorrowful. Information was going out, but she seemed unable to grasp anything except the fact that her beloved brother-in-law lay dead in the library.

She found herself wanting Ben desperately. If she could feel his solid presence beside her, his arm about her shoulders, she might be able to take hold with something like her old authority. She needed to feel his hand, hear his voice, for she couldn't even find tears.

Dry and empty, she seemed drained of will and strength. Emanuel was speaking again, but she had stopped hearing. Leaning her head back against the leather chair back, she closed her eyes.

After what seemed a long time, she felt a touch at her elbow. She opened her eyes to find her son's round face level with her own. He looked sober but not frightened.

'Uncle Hanni's sick,' he said. 'I went to the liberry to put back a book, and he's on the floor and he won't talk to me.'

'Oh, God!' she sighed. 'Why didn't I lock the door behind me? What was I thinking about, not to make sure Benjie couldn't get back in there?'

Father Clarrington came into the room, though she hadn't known when he left it. He looked at her, at Benjie. Then he bent and took the child's hand. 'Come with Grandpa, my boy. Yes, I know about Uncle Hannibal. We've called the doctor and your daddy. Now you must go up to your room, for your Mama isn't feeling very well, right now.' He bent to kiss the ruddy cheek.

'I'll come up and tell you all about it, while we go. Do you want to help Grandpa pull himself up all those steps? Fine. We'll get Hildy to fix you milk toast and hot chocolate, and you can have your supper on the little dishes in the school-room.' He had a genius for managing children, and without protest the little boy went with him.

Thankfully, Marise watched them leave the room. Then she squeezed her eyes shut and forced her mind to work again. Her family needed her. Letting herself go into shock wasn't going to help anyone or anything, herself least of all.

She didn't quite understand why Hannibal's death had shaken her so badly, even unexpected as it was. But she had been very fond of the big man, dependent on his steady good sense and undeviating calm.

She pulled herself out of the chair and made sure she was steady on her feet. A nurse must not be guilty of letting go as she had just done. It was weak and self-indulgent. She turned to the door, went through into the corridor, and stepped into the library again before she could change her mind.

There was a faint odor in the room, familiar, for she had attended many deaths. She forced herself to cross the Persian rug to the table and round its end to kneel beside Hannibal's body. She should have checked it before now, even though she knew without a doubt that he was dead.

It should be done as a matter of form. She touched the wrist, which was not yet entirely cold, though it had lost the warmth of living flesh. The eyeballs were fixed, the irises without reaction. There could be no doubt.

His expression puzzled her. Pain made strange things happen, sometimes, at the end of a life, but why should he have looked so stunned with surprise? This was not the surprise that the sudden agony of a heart attack should cause, even though there had been no warning of any heart trouble before.

He looked just as if he had glanced up

from what he was doing and seen something so unexpected and alarming that it sent him into shock. But in this solid house, filled with loving people, that was an impossibility.

Kneeling there, she looked beneath the table, seeing the long wooden footrest that ran its length, between columnar legs with lion-paw feet. Something glinted against the garnet, purple, and blue of the carpet. She rose and went around the table.

When she looked down, she found it was only a hair clasp. But it was not hers. All of hers were pale to match her hair. This was black, and caught in it was a long strand of black hair, like Ben's hair and Hanni's. There was no black-haired woman in the house, and no one had visited them in weeks.

Without asking herself why, she put the clasp in her pocket. Then she heard the voice, that thin, childish voice, singing a tuneless melody. From where?

She stared about her, but it was impossible to place it. She shivered and ran out of the room, locking the door behind her.

★ ★ ★

She still shuddered when she thought of that day. It had marked the first break in the happy current of their lives, the first irreparable loss. Long ago she had moved the library table to cover the spot where Hannibal had lain, but it didn't really help.

She could still see those shocked black eyes, flat with death, but still holding the terrible surprise that had triggered the last wild spasm of his heart. Was it that which had shaken his mind from its moorings?

Marise took a stack of books from the small table near the door and returned them neatly to their places. Then she began choosing others. If she lived to be eighty, she would never be able to devour that entire collection of books, which was a comfort.

Stacking her new choices, she went to kneel beside the shelf that still held Ben's childish books. With a gentle finger, she touched their backs. *The Jungle Books. The Wind in the Willows.*

She felt tears rising behind her eyes, and she rose abruptly and turned away.

Of all her losses, those of Ben and Benjie were still too painful to bear. She took up her books and, once more, locked the library door behind her.

* * *

The man felt that his surveillance was becoming too obvious. He had been watching for a week now, without any attempt at concealment. He had hoped to attract the notice of the woman who had to live in that house, but there wasn't the slightest hint she knew he was there.

Others were not so blind.

More than one person living in the neighborhood had stopped to inquire if he were looking for some specific address. He managed to disarm suspicion by claiming to be an insurance investigator, checking the place out before his company wrote a new policy. Or a former tenant's child, looking at his old home. He had no trouble with telling any number of inventive and persuasive lies, but he knew he had become too noticeable.

He approached a rooming house down the street that had been converted from an old mansion. Like most of those along Myrtle Street, it had left behind the days of large families and readily available servants and now was cut up into many small apartments, two or three rooms set into what had been a single large one. Though the exterior walls were solid stone, thick and impervious, he found, once he was installed, that the new partitions were thin enough to hear through.

This was better than watching, for the old couple who owned the house had nothing much to do to occupy their days, and the two discussed every person walking down the street. Most local automobiles were intimately known, for Myrtle was a cul-de-sac, and each one that moved along the street was described, its possible destination surmised, and its driver dissected as to character, profession, and possible flaws.

Sitting in the grim room he had rented, he had heard his landlady tell her husband, 'The Trustee is late this month. He usually goes to see the Widow about the tenth, and here it is the twelfth and he hasn't been yet. I just know she doesn't eat enough, there alone. That boy hasn't come with her groceries, either. You don't suppose she's died in there, all by herself, do you?'

'Now, Ellie, if she had we'd have seen some kind of activity going on. They've got to check on her regularly, and we'd have seen police cars or an ambulance, I'm sure and certain. No, she's all right. And don't think about going over there to inquire about her health. You remember how short she cut you off the last time.'

The cracked voice said, 'Well, I still think it'd be the neighborly thing to do. You know, she's still a handsome woman. It's odd, because you'd think that living alone like she does she'd let herself go. But no, she's still got the figure of a girl. Her hair's the prettiest pale blonde, clean and shiny, though all done up in a knot on top of her head.

'She doesn't wear a smidge of makeup, but I have to admit she doesn't need it.

Skin like cream. You'd think all she went through would have left her looking like a beat-up old woman, but it hasn't. Makes you wonder . . . '

'Ellie, if the police and the District Attorney and the sheriff, all together, couldn't find any reason to suspect her, you know damn well there was nothing to suspect. Let it alone. The poor woman has lost everybody she ever had and didn't even have any kin of her own. I don't blame her a mite for just shutting herself in and letting the world go to hell. I'd like to do the same myself, from time to time, if I could afford to.'

At that point they moved away and left him to ponder what he had heard. So she still looked the same, did she? And she was still forthright to the point of bluntness.

That was interesting. Eventually, she was going to make his long wait worth while. If, of course, he ever found a way to get into that solid stone fortress of hers.

★ ★ ★

As Marise moved about the house on her regular cleaning rounds, she found herself assaulted continually by bits and pieces of the past. No matter how securely she bolted the doors of her mind, from time to time a sudden glimpse of a room, the odor of leather or lemon polish or disinfectant could send her back in an instant, into those grim years that followed Hannibal's death.

At least once a year she cleaned faithfully, from the rooms that had been used on the third floor, right down to the basement. The first floor took most of her time, for she used the kitchen and the library, and she liked to keep the parlor nice for the Trustee's visits, as well as the monthly deliveries of the young clerk who brought her supplies. She always served them cookies and tea or coffee there.

The second floor was not quite as well kept, and she frequently felt guilty about that. When cleaning there, she always began with Father Clarrington's room, for it still felt like home to her. She had sat there with him every day, after his stroke. She read to him, wrote letters to his old associates, clients, or distant kin, took notes for the guidance of the Trust that was assuming partial control of Clarrington Enterprises.

The corporation was too much for Ben, even with her help. She had turned over much of the management of the farm to a young man she had hired soon after taking over, though she still kept the overall planning firmly in her own hands. But the Trust managed the business end of the corporation, leaving Ben free to work with his beloved trees.

Days and weeks and months overlapped in that room. Every time she went into it she was assaulted with many images. Father Clarrington sitting in the deep chair, smiling as she brought Benjie in for a morning visit, before Hannibal's death brought the stroke and devastating old age upon the old man. The high bed they had installed to make caring for him easier still sat in its corner. So many things . . .

★　★　★

She'd tapped lightly on the white-painted door. 'Come in,' he said, his tone thin and light as that of a ghost. 'Oh, Daughter, come sit beside me and talk a bit. I've worn out my patience with my book. Don't let them bring me any more bestsellers, will you? Those idiots can't write! To somebody who cut his teeth on Faulkner and Wolfe, this is nothing but drivel. I have no interest in the personal problems of a brainless advertising executive.'

She laughed as she took the abused book. 'I do agree. I'll bring you *Watership Down*. That's one of your favorites, even if it bears no resemblance whatsoever to Faulkner. Or perhaps it does, in a way.' She had a sudden thought.

'Would you like to reread Dickens? I think he might suit your mood, for he had such a gritty sense of people and the world they lived in.'

He reached for her hand and his thin fingers tightened about it. His black eyes, gazing up from a pillow that was only just paler than his face, thanked her for her cheerfulness and apologized wordlessly for his predicament. Neither spoke, but he managed a smile.

She had gone away to pick out a stack of books to amuse him; most of those she read aloud to him, when he became too weak to hold them in his trembling hands. She'd been reading aloud on the day Benjie went exploring onto the third floor.

The child's light steps hadn't broken into her concentration, but her father-in-law seemed to have preternatural senses when it came to that part of the house. He broke into her reading. 'Marri, someone has gone up the stair and down the third floor corridor. I think it must be Benjie. Will you look?' He was paper-white. 'I don't want him to come to any harm, and I don't want him troubled by . . . anything out of the past. Besides, the floor is getting to be spongy up there. Hildy told me.'

She dropped her book and hurried up to see. She had no wish for her son to ask any questions about that unused part of the house, any more than her father-in-law had wanted it when she asked for herself. The thought of the horror story he told her still haunted her at times, though her sound and sturdy child belied any hint of abnormality.

Whatever happened in the last generation but one was over and done with, she was certain. But still she wanted no dark memories dredged up from the past.

Marise peered down the corridor, which was dark, because the bulbs were out in the tulip lamps that should have lit it and the draperies were closed over the window at the far end past the angle. No small figure was to be seen. That meant Benjie, if it was he, had gone down the cross passage, and she had never been down that way.

Hildy's warnings and her own promise had kept her from exploring this part of the house, particularly after she heard the old tales. She dreaded the thought of her bright, sunny-natured child poking about in those musty depths.

Marise hurried over the dusty carpet without looking at the doors on either side. The cross passage went the depth of a single room to her right, and she checked that before examining the long leg of the passage to the left. At the end of the way she could see movement, almost invisible in the shadows.

'Benjie?' she called. She moved toward the small shape in the shadows. 'Come to Mama, dear. You shouldn't be up here alone. Hildy says there are spiders.'

He came, but very slowly, stopping once to look back at the door that was part of the dead end of the corridor.

'Come on, Sweetheart. We'll go visit Grampa. He was asking for you.' She held out her hand.

He moved then, rushing along the passage to bump his head against her side like a young calf. 'It's dark up here, Mama. Why do they keep the curtain closed? Why are all the doors locked? It's sort of scary up here.'

She gathered him against her in a hug. 'Well, Ben, we don't need all these rooms. It would cost a lot of money to fix them up and keep them clean. What would be the use of doing that, just to please a lot of spiders and mice? Nobody wants to look at dusty carpets and cobwebby ceilings, so we keep the curtains closed so they won't show if anyone comes up so far. See?' She was rather proud of her spur-of-the-moment invention.

That had seemed to be the end of it, yet something about her son's visit to those forbidden passages had disturbed her and given her nightmares that lasted, intermittently, for years afterward. Indeed, they had recurred until the ultimate horror that ended it all.

She shook herself and returned to the present to take up her dust mop. The hospital bed loomed against the wall, and she ran the mop along the edge of the hardwood flooring beneath it. A thin coat of dust had settled there since her last visit. But she still felt chilled, for the thought of her nightmare persisted.

The first night after her son's climb to the third floor she had dreamed hideous things. A voice, distant but very clear, had spoken to her. Hideous things. Hateful, hating words.

'You don't belong here,' it had said. 'I will not have you here! I tried to show you that, when you first came, and you didn't understand. This is my family. This is my house. You are an intruder, an outsider. You're not a Clarrington, with your fair hair and blue eyes.

'Even Hildy makes a fuss over you, and Father and Mother Clarrington do, too. Ben does, and Hannibal did. Oh, yes, Hannibal did! But I fixed him, or made him fix himself, which is the same thing.'

The voice had gone on and on, thin and whining and terrifying, while she had struggled to wake. But she hadn't been able to, try as she might. The worst had come at the end of that nightmare.

'I'll get the child. I like children. You can't take him with you when you go, but you will, oh, you will go!'

At last she was able to shake off sleep and get to her feet, there in the round bedroom she shared with Ben. He slept deeply, exhausted by his hard work in the woods and the mills. But she stood there, soaked with sweat in her damp night-gown, listening. She strained to hear, as if she might go on hearing that demonic voice, even while awake.

Strangely enough, even at the time she

had not felt fear. It had not been one of those dreams that makes you afraid of falling asleep again because it might continue. No, she had been angry.

Nobody, real or imaginary, was going to force her out of her home and away from the family that had become hers as truly as if she had been born into it. And nobody was going to get her child!

She had gone back to sleep quite peacefully and dreamed no more that night. But for years the dream came intermittently, leaving her angry every time. It had come, she remembered, on the night before Father Clarrington died.

She'd been reading aloud that evening, with Benjie tucked up in her lap, though he was getting to be a bit large for her to hold. He had been seven, already in school, but he still loved to sit and listen to Shakespeare and Dickens and Thoreau, while she read to his Grampa.

It had been a warm evening, and the windows were open. Though he had become very weak, Father Clarrington had seemed to feel rather well, his eyes twinkling at the funny passages. He had reached out, from time to time, to touch his grandson's bare knee.

They read until Ben came in from the woods. Then she kissed the old man good night and took Benjie away to his room. After that she went to take Ben's late supper out of the warming oven, for Hildy tired more easily, now, and she needed more and more help with her work.

Ben was in high spirits. The mills were busy, and his theories on replanting the selectively cut forests were proving to be sound ones. The two of them had talked far into the night and they fell asleep at last, between sentences.

But after a few hours she waked. This was not a dream, she felt certain. The voice was there, that same hateful voice and the same hateful words.

This time Marise was not disoriented with sleep. She knew someone was speaking to her, standing on the landing outside her sitting room door. There had been no doubt in her mind as she threw on a robe and clattered down the six steps into the round room below.

It took a moment to unfasten the bolt on the door, but she hurried as much as possible. Yet when she looked out into the dim-lit stairway, there was no one in sight. She stood there, panting, shaking with fury, and listened intently. Perhaps it had been at that point her mind began playing tricks on her.

She did not sleep well the rest of that night. Something besides the abrupt waking troubled her, and she rose early, leaving Ben to sleep late. Hildy, too, was late, so Marise prepared breakfast for herself.

As Hildy still didn't appear, she made trays for the rest of the household, too, putting food for Mother Clarrington and Miss Edenson into the warming oven. Then she took the tray with milk toast, weak tea, and jam and went up the stair to Father Clarrington's door.

Her tap was not answered, so she opened the door gently to see if he was still asleep. At first she thought he was.

'Father? Are you awake? I've brought your breakfast,' she had whispered.

Setting the tray carefully on the bedside

table, she turned and bent over the still shape on the bed. His eyes were closed, quite peacefully, and one pale hand lay outside the covers. She could see the tracks of needles marking the thin arm, and she thought of all the shots she had given him for his pain. The cyanosis dyeing his skin was clear.

Tears came to her eyes, and she pulled the sheet over his face before realizing that this unattended death must be investigated by the Coroner. So she put things back as they were and stepped back.

This time she behaved like a professional. No vaporings, no numbness, as she had experienced with Hannibal's death. Yet the pain was no less real. And she knew she must call Ben at once.

He had been devastated. She had known how close he felt to his father, but she hadn't quite realized the depth of his feeling, particularly since Ben lost his brother. Yet her husband pulled himself together, called the doctor, the coroner, and did everything right. All the time she could see him bleeding quietly inside.

Together, they went to see his mother, which had been the most painful thing she had ever had to do, up to that time. As they moved up the stair, Ben touched her shoulder.

'Did you give Dad a shot last night?'

She thought backward. Sometimes it was hard to recall whether she remembered if it had been that night or a week ago, so regular was the routine. Then she called to mind the chart, which she kept as meticulously as if she had been working in a hospital.

'No,' she said. 'He seemed to be fairly free of pain, for once, and I just gave him his sleeping pill. No shot. Why do you ask?'

'I found this on the floor. I almost stepped on it, in fact. Is it the kind you've been using?' He held out a syringe with a disposable barrel, still attached. There was the residue of something sticky inside the barrel.

Marise took it and held it to the nearest lamp. 'It's an unused one from the cabinet,' she said. 'I always dispose of the empties after I use one. With a child in the house, it's the only safe thing to do.' Then the impact of his question hit her.

'Ben, nobody could have ... would have ... '

He was pale, his black eyes burning. 'There's something we must talk over, later. I didn't think it would ever be necessary, but now I know better. There is someone who would and could, if there was an opportunity.' He groaned softly and put his arm about her shoulders.

'We should have told you, right off. We just hoped ... We hoped the problem would never come to light or that it would go away. You'll understand later, when I tell you.'

Miss Edenson had just finished brushing Elizabeth Clarrington's hair for the morning, and the invalid was sitting upright in bed, her back propped, her knees elevated to help her circulation. She looked like a doll that some child had arranged and then gone away and forgotten.

When she looked toward the door and saw the two of them coming, she went even paler than usual. Edenson's glance followed her patient's, and the nurse went quickly to the woman's side and turned to face them. She seemed ready to protect her charge from some sort of attack.

'Mother.' Ben took her hand and touched her hair. Then he looked questioningly at the nurse. 'Mother, I have something sad to tell you. Dad's gone. In the night. Marise found him just a few minutes ago, when she took his breakfast in. We've called everyone necessary, and you don't have to worry about anything except staying well yourself.'

Elizabeth Clarrington closed her eyes tightly for a long moment. Then she opened them and said, 'Was it a . . . natural death?'

Marise jumped. That was a strange question, knowing how ill the old man had been for so long. It was not a question she would have expected from her mother-in-law, particularly at such a time.

Ben's answer was even more of a shock. 'I don't think so, Mother. I found a needle on the floor. There was something still in the barrel, and I'm going to have

Mark get somebody in the lab to analyze it.'

Mrs. Clarrington let out a ragged breath that sounded almost like a death rattle. 'I've known for years she could get out, Ben. Not always, and we never knew exactly how she manages to, but she does get out.

'Hannibal wouldn't believe me when I told him, and I think that killed him. Your father didn't want to believe, and it has probably killed him too. She won't rest until she has done her worst. You know it and I know it. You have to tell Marise.'

She was turning blue, even as she spoke.

'Edenson!' Marise said. 'Her medicine! Quickly!'

The nurse moved with accustomed speed, and soon the shot was easing the attack. Once his mother was asleep, Ben took his wife's hand and led her away. Marise had dreaded hearing what he was going to say, for in some way she felt it endangered everything she knew and cherished.

And it did. Indeed, it did.

Marise had spent a good part of the intervening years trying to forget or suppress the memory of what Ben told her, when they reached their snug sitting room at last. The happiness she had known in the tower apartment was too precious to allow it to be tainted by the terrible thing her husband had said.

Even after the last anguished confrontation there, a major act of will allowed Marise to continue living where she had lived with Ben. She still might turn, sometimes, to envision his face there, hear his voice.

But then he had been almost as pale as his father. He stood before the tiny hearth, facing the rocking chair in which he had placed her. She knew from the tension in his hands and neck how hard it was for him to speak.

'We've been cowards. Cowards and fools and villains,' he began. 'I suspected it from the first, but when you're faced with the kind of agony this family has known for generations, you don't always do the wise thing.

'You asked me once why I stayed away from home for so long before I got sick and you saved my life and gave me the courage to come back here. You could see at once that the bunk I told you about quarrelling with my father wasn't true. I saw it in your eyes.

'No, it wasn't problems with Hanni or Father or Mother or Aunt Lina that drove me away. There was another reason, one that affected me more than anyone else in the family, I was sure, though now that seems egocentric. Everyone suffered, and I was the only one to run away.'

Marise stretched her hand toward him, trying to touch, to comfort him. 'Why, Ben? I have begun to suspect, but the time has come for hard facts, not intuition. Is there still someone locked up there in that third floor room?'

He took her extended hand and gripped it tightly. 'Yes.' He swallowed loudly, unable to say more for a moment.

His fingers tightened painfully around hers. She looked up quietly, waiting, though dread filled her. She breathed deeply, trying to remain calm, while her husband regained his control.

'Who is it? Ben, I can see you've kept it back so forcefully that it's almost impossible for you to get the words out now, but the time has come. Not only for me; we have to do our best for Benjie too.'

Color was coming back into his face as he sighed. 'Right. I'll put it to you straight. I, too, had a twin. A sister. That was why mother had such a hard time with the birth, why it strained her heart almost fatally.'

Marise understood at once. 'Once your mother said she'd had a little girl, but I assumed that was a stillbirth.'

He shook his dark head. 'No. A double birth. Benjamin and Penelope. Two dark-eyed children who lived the first few years of their lives together as only twins can seem to do, thinking together, acting together. We adored each other . . . or at least I adored her. There's no way to be certain what her feelings for me might have been. Not now.

'Like so many in our family, we were

bright, healthy, happy. We were hard-headed, of course, as all Clarringtons seem to be, mad or sane. But we seemed normal, whatever that is. For years things were fine. Then we began school. I loved it, but Pen hated it from the first day.'

Marise sat quietly, waiting. That was all she could do to make this easier for him.

'They put us in different classrooms, which seemed to be their policy with twins. They'd found, I learned later, that it made for greater independence for both children, which seems sensible. I missed Pen, naturally, but there was so much to do, so many children to get to know, new things to learn that I didn't make a fuss. We had plenty of time together after school.

'I thought she was having as much fun as I was.' He stared out of the window, across the garden below, where tree shadows streaked the grass with purple. 'Right down there beside the rockery I learned the truth.

'"They don't want me any more!" she yelled at me. 'They've taken me away from home and away from you, and they've put me with dumb kids who don't like me.'

'I tried every argument I'd heard our parents use for going to school, but she didn't listen, to me or to anyone else. Ever. Anything that didn't conform to her iron convictions of what was right, which meant what *she* wanted, never penetrated her skull.

'She called me a traitor. She thought that I belonged to her totally, body and mind. I had no right to enjoy school alone, to know any child except her, to play games she refused to learn. When I objected, she picked up a rock off the rockery and tried to brain me with it. We were seven years old, Marri.'

She stood and took him in her arms. His head came down and she felt his cheek against her hair. Tears trickled onto her scalp.

'Of course you told your parents!' she said.

'I ran for my life. Father was in his study with the manager of the lumber mills. When he looked up to see me standing in the door, wild-eyed, with a bruise the size of an egg on my forehead, he dismissed the fellow almost rudely. The first time I ever saw him short with anyone in my life.

'Then he took me on his lap. I felt him shaking when I told him what happened. That was when he told me about Clara. About them all, the warped, twisted Clarringtons going all the way back to the old country. He warned me of the flaw in our genes that made it dangerous to have children at all, even though those without the taint were usually fine people.'

He held her at arm's length and looked into her eyes. He was solemn, his eyes shadowed with concern. 'Marri, I needed you, wanted you. If that damn doctor hadn't been convinced I'd be sterile and told me so, I'd have told you at once so we could take precautions. Before we married, of course, because I'm not that big a fool or a villain. But I thought we had time — years, he said, it might be before we had to think about having children.

'We'd already talked it out, and you seemed content that there might not be

111

children at all. I thought we were safe.'

'We are,' she said. All the conviction she could muster strengthened her voice. 'Benjie is fine and sane and normal. There never was a healthier child, one more balanced and cheerful than he is. Don't torture yourself with impossibilities, Ben. Not with all the rest of the pain you've been handling alone. Why didn't you let me help you?'

He shook his head. 'We never said anything among ourselves, even. It wasn't exactly a conspiracy of silence, keeping you from learning our secret. It was more the fact that all of us loved you and wanted you to be happy, without a cloud on your horizon.

'You seemed so content and so confident that we couldn't bear to do anything to spoil things for you. And then when there was the baby coming, without warning and against all the odds, it was too late.

'That would have been a dreadful worry for a pregnant woman, one you didn't need to have to cope with. I know you too well to think you'd have considered an abortion, and without that option there was no point in telling you. I think you may agree with me there.'

She nodded, understanding without agreeing at all. But there was no need to trouble him further.

'To this day, Penelope lives in that room up on the third floor. The one the young man killed himself in. The same one where Clara strangled her mother and died at the hands of her father.'

Marise shivered. 'No wonder Hildy nearly fainted when I said I'd go exploring back along that corridor. No wonder Father had his ear cocked in that direction, listening for any sound Benjie might make if he explored the upper story. How you could all live with such horror in your lives without showing the strain. I can't understand it.'

'We've been doing it for generations,' Ben said. He sounded infinitely sad and weary.

Then Marise thought of the implications of her mother-in-law's words earlier. 'Ben, how does she get out? Your mother said she has known it for years. How could she escape from a third floor room with barred windows and, I would think, locks on the outside of the door?'

Ben shook his head. 'We've tried and tried and never figured it out. We thought that had stopped, for it didn't happen for years. Then when Hanni died, I felt in my gut he'd come face to face with her and the shock was too much for him. There's no telling what she said or did to kick him over the edge.

'We've had Andy watching the door every night since you came. That seemed to work for a long time, but you know that Andy is getting worse all the time. He used to be able to function normally even when he was drunk. Now he's not handling it very well, but he's so terrified of her he'd never neglect to check the locks. I just can't think how she got out.'

Marise felt the blood drain from her face. 'Benjie went up there once, years ago. Father heard him, somehow, and sent me to check. Benjie was almost to the door down at the end of the cross corridor. He seemed to be fascinated by it, though I couldn't see too well. It's very dark up there. What if he unfastened a lock? Just through curiosity? She might have gotten out then . . . '

Ben closed his eyes. 'Father could always hear a fly walking on the ceiling. Thank God he could hear a little boy's feet on a carpeted stair. I don't want to think about what might have happened if he hadn't. For that is Pen's door, and it has bolts on the outside, not locks.' He opened his eyes again and stared at her, but he was seeing something inside his own mind.

'Mother has always been terrified of fire. She was afraid that if the house caught, Pen might burn to death while somebody searched for keys. A child could open that door from the outside.'

★   ★   ★

Now, standing in the middle of her sitting room, Marise felt a long shudder shake her middle-aged bones. They had been so certain that they could manage the problem and keep Benjie safe.

They had bundled Benjie off to school,

as if things were normal, then went at once to the upper floor and checked the bolts on Ben's sister's door.

But the bolts had been fastened. The moment Ben touched the wood, sliding the top bolt back and forth to check it, a voice sounded from the other side.

'Who's tapping at my door?' The tone was light and childish, and Marise felt sure that was the voice she had heard when she thought herself going round the bend.

Ben answered firmly. 'Only Ben, Penny. I'm just checking to see everything is secure. Andy will bring up your breakfast soon. Do you need any new painting supplies?' His face was taut, the lines from cheekbone to chin deep and agonized.

'I need alizarin crimson,' came the reply from beyond the door. 'And viridian. You might get some more of those canvas panels, the ones that are already stretched. It's easier than doing it myself, but mind you get the good canvas, not the cheap kind.'

'I'll make sure it's done. Take care, dear.' Even in the poor light of the shadowy hall, Ben looked suddenly old, as he turned to leave.

Marise felt a jolt of pity, for the girl as well as for Ben. 'She is talented too? Like the musician and poor little Clara?'

He plodded beside her as if infinitely weary. When he spoke it was quietly, with an undertone of tragedy. 'Yes she is. Fantastically. Father has sent some of her work to an agent in New York, and it's in a gallery there right now. We sell a piece from time to time and put it into a trust for her.

'Her work is . . . an acquired taste. It's frightening, but it's also bright and fierce and compelling. She has a growing following, believe it or not, and critics have been wildly enthusiastic, on occasion. We have spread the story that she is crippled and housebound. That isn't much of a lie, is it?' He smiled crookedly.

★　★　★

In her lonely present, Marise shivered. Would those memories never fade and leave her to do the same?

5

As she went about the house on her regular cleaning run, every door held a memory that distressed Marise. There was not one she disliked opening more than the door to Hannibal's bedroom; not even the library held sadder memories, though she had seldom opened that door when her brother-in-law was alive. Hannibal was one of those vital, busy people who keep moving unless very ill or sound asleep. Their frequent conversations had taken place principally in the parlor in the evenings or in the library, and she recalled them with pleasure. He had an acute mind, full of odd facts and unexpected observations. Every exchange with him was one from which Marise came away feeling she had learned something valuable.

As his work dealt with the legal and investment aspects of the Clarrington business enterprise, he had done most of his work at home. The law office he maintained in downtown Channing was for his private practice, which he cheerfully neglected, leaving much of the work to his young partner. Nevertheless, she knew he had stayed on top of all his cases, and she knew that Hanni had possessed that brilliant 'edge' Ben had, though it was focused in a different direction.

Once Hanni had said, 'Ben is a genius with trees and growing things. He seems to feel sap in his veins, instead of blood, and he can tell when a blight is taking hold of a piece of timber land before any outward sign can be found. The foresters marvel at him.' He'd laughed his rich laugh.

'He can also feel what the housing market is going to do before either lenders or builders have a clue. I don't have a scrap of that sort of intuition, though I use his constantly in our work. I'm just a stodgy old lawyer, incapable of flights of brilliance.'

That wasn't true, of course. Hanni had a sense of people to rival Ben's understanding of growing things. Though he never mentioned any names, her brother-in-law told wild tales about his clients' affairs, his comments cutting to the bone.

'If I could make him see why he's behaving like a four star ass, I think he'd straighten up,' he said of one young millionaire who was about to take on his seventh liability for alimony.

'I've decided people don't want to behave sanely. I've come to the conclusion that sanity is completely out of style, though perhaps one with my heredity shouldn't say such a thing.'

Marise remembered laughing in spite of herself. Who except Hanni would have joked about his family's history? But if she had known at the time how very tragic that was, she would never have laughed, she now knew.

That conversation had taken place in the library, of course, but now she must go into his empty bedroom to clean, and she hated the thought. It had been there she had met Penelope, face to face, for the first time.

Hannibal had been dead for four years,

Father Clarrington for two. Benjie had been almost nine, growing very quickly and making a start at becoming as tall as his father and grandfather. To her satisfaction, he had seemed sturdier than either, and she could see a hint of her own father's solid squareness in his small body.

At that time Marise was in her mid-thirties, still soundly convinced of her own health and sanity. She had taken on as much of the household duties as she could manage, along with the farm and her family, and she made it a point to visit her mother-in-law as often as possible.

Hildy was getting feeble, and rheumatism had begun to bother her badly, the pain affecting her disposition. She even snapped at Andy, when he ventured into her kitchen. Once she even lost her temper with Benjie, which told Marise how much pain troubled the old cook.

Marise had volunteered to clean the upper floors of the house, though she never bothered with the unused rooms. That would have been foolish, given the short-handed condition of the household. What was done there, Andy did without mention or supervision. She also carried up her mother-in-law's meals on the occasions when Miss Edenson was away or was too busy to come down after them.

While upstairs, she usually inspected a few chambers for damp, dust, and the mildew that crept into walls and carpets because of the damp southern climate. It had been on such an errand that she came into Hannibal's room, using the key she now carried in the pocket of her coverall.

To her shock and dismay, she found someone inside the room she been certain would be empty. A tall, stocky woman, black-haired and black-eyed, stood there. She was dressed in faded jeans and a paint-smeared smock. It could only be Penelope, and Marise felt sudden terror as those sharp eyes skewered her, inspecting her from head to heel.

She was speechless, backing away toward the door, when the woman spoke. 'Where is my brother Hannibal? This is his room, and even if he's out, his things should be here. Who're you? The new maid?'

Then the black eyes narrowed. 'No. You're the one who drove him away, aren't you? You took my brother Ben away from me too. I knew you would as soon as I heard about you.' Her voice grew shrill with fury.

'You took my Ben. You took my father. You are taking away my home every day, and now you have done something to get rid of Hanni. You're an evil, wicked woman. I heard all about you from Andy, just after Hildy read the telegram.

'He knows about women like you who nurse rich men and get them into their clutches and marry them. And don't look so innocent; you can't fool me, though you do seem to lead the rest around by their noses.'

Marise watched her as she backed very slowly and cautiously toward the open door. She tried to smile, but her face was so stiff it felt it might crack with the effort. She had to say something, pretend things were safe and normal, or who knew what this mad woman might do?

She gauged the distance left between her and the doorway. 'Ben tells me you are a fine painter,' she ventured. She took another soft step backward. 'He says your work sells well in New York. I would love to see some of your paintings some time.' She knew she was babbling, but her tongue seemed to have taken over the task of concealing her fear.

Penelope looked down at her disdainfully. Her raven wing brows rose sardonically. 'Don't think you can flatter me. I am totally above that sort of thing, and the only reason I don't choke the life out of you at once is the fact that you gave Ben a son.'

Marise felt herself jerk, though she tried to control it.

'Don't flinch. I know about Benjie. I know about everything that goes on in this house, from top to bottom, and nobody can keep me from finding out what I want to learn. They've tried for years to keep me locked away in my room all the time, but they've never figured out how I manage to get out. I get out whenever I want to, remember that.

'Yes, Marise, I know all about your son. I like little boys, and I see him playing in the garden on fine days. He's a lot like my Ben was at the same age. When I want him, he'll be mine. Just wait and see.' She laughed, a low chuckle that held great humor and charm.

'Ben was mine, you know,' she said. 'Hanni was too old, too big, too grown up. I couldn't manage him the way I could my twin. Hanni was cruel to me, you know. He bought all new locks, and it took me ages to learn how to get out again. When you came he used to check my door every day, so nothing I did was any good.

'He stood outside and sang your praises until I nearly went mad. I hated Hannibal, you know. I still do, but he's my brother. A Clarrington. He belongs to me, like it or not. What have you done with him?'

She moved toward Marise, sheer menace in her expression. Marise backed another step toward the refuge of the hallway behind her, but she knew it was too late to run. She had to use shock tactics.

'Penelope, Hannibal is dead. Don't you remember? I suspect it might have been you who surprised him in the library. He wouldn't have expected to see you, after taking such care to keep you confined. He must have inherited your mother's bad heart, though nobody seemed to suspect it. He died in the library, whether or not you were there.'

Penelope laughed. The sound brought Marise's neck-hairs upright.

'I did give him such a start,' she crooned. 'Poor Hanni thought he had me fixed at last. He was so sure I was locked away and forgotten and helpless. He didn't count on . . . ' she stopped short and peered suspiciously at Marise. 'But I mustn't give away my little secrets, now must I?' she asked, her tone sickeningly coy.

Marise found her fear replaced by anger. 'That shock killed your brother, so it was you who sent him away, not I. It was I who found him lying on the carpet, his hands on his chest. His eyes were filled with astonishment, though I didn't know what could have caused it at the time. Now I do know.'

'He thought he had me safe and sound, but that was not entirely true. I was a surprise, but the thing I told him was much, much worse. I will never forget his face.' Again that laugh chilled Marise to the marrow.

'So he died? Yes, I seem to remember now. There was a funeral downstairs. I heard everything that was said, you know. Nothing can be kept from me. The ducts run through the walls, up and down.' Penelope sidled closer, for now she too seemed to have thought of the open door. 'I'm faster than you, faster than anyone. You can't get to the corridor before I do, and if you run I'll catch you. I get . . . excited when I chase people. A little girl ran from me once, and I got excited. That was when they locked me up in that room on the third floor. I hate those bars!'

Frightened as she had been, Marise felt a stab of sudden pity for her sister-in-law. None of this was any of her doing. Those greedy ancestors back in the old country had sowed a shocking crop, and their unfortunate descendants must harvest it, like it or not.

With cold certainty, Marise knew she stood in mortal danger. The woman was set to explode like a bomb. Calculating her chances, Marise whirled and fled through the door to the sanctuary of the corridor. She barely made it, for Penelope's heavy body slammed into the door just behind her, as she turned to lock it.

She couldn't hold it shut. She felt it wrenched from her grasp and jerked open from inside. Marise gasped and ran, shouting for help. Hildy and her husband were far away downstairs, deafened by circumstance and alcohol. But Edenson was nearby, though the nurse might not come to her aid.

As Marise neared Mother Clarrington's door, it opened and the nurse's face appeared in the crack. 'Help me!' she panted. 'Penelope's loose, and she's after me. I think she intends to kill me.'

Edenson scowled and shut the door with a snap, almost in Marise's face. The sound brought her to her wits, and she paused in mid-flight.

Marise turned to face her pursuer. Not for nothing was she trained in one of the best nursing schools in New England. She knew how to handle the heaviest invalid, the most violent delirium. She knew how to deal with madmen.

Penelope, seeing her stop, slowed cautiously, warily. She was much taller and heavier than Marise, though, and that seemed to reassure her. She lunged forward at last, hands out, reaching.

Marise sidestepped neatly, tripping her antagonist with one knee, and slammed her elbow behind the big woman's neck as she bent to catch her balance. Penelope went down with a thud.

Stubborn anger coursed through Marise's veins. She didn't wait for help. Instead she reached for the big vase that sat outside Mrs. Clarrington's door and caught it up in one hand, though the weight should have been prohibitive.

She swung it around and heard it shatter against Penelope's skull with a crunch. At last the woman slumped at her feet, unconscious or nearly so.

The sound of feet on the stairs caught

Marise's ear, and she moved to the head of the flight. Andy was rolling upward drunkenly, and a gasping Hildy followed him.

'Marri! Did Pen . . . ?' Hildy's voice trailed off as she reached the corridor and saw the mess near Mrs. Clarrington's door. 'My God! Is she dead?'

Marise still remembered leaning against the ivory wall. 'No,' she'd said. 'She's just knocked out. I found her in Hannibal's room, and she accused me of driving him away. Then she admitted she had surprised him in the library. She may or may not remember that he died, though I told her just now. I think things come and go in her mind. She wanted to kill me, and I ran.' She'd stared at Mother Clarrington's door with some bitterness. 'Don't ever call on Edenson for help. She slammed the door in my face, when I called out.'

Hildy frowned. 'I think it is because you are a nurse, and she feels you might take her work from her.' Hildy bent over the unconscious woman. 'Andy, you come here this moment. We must get her into her own place before she wake up. Much trouble there will be if she is awake. You agree?' She asked Marise.

'I do agree. Let me help you lift her. Andy, you reach under her other side. Hildy doesn't need to lug all this weight up a flight of stairs. Ready? Now!' She heaved, and they got the heavy body up, catching her under the arms from either side.

They started upward, Penelope's feet dragging, toes down, on the carpet. They left a pair of furrows in the velvety nap, Marise noticed, glancing back. It was a steep climb and she felt her breath failing before they reached the top. Then down the long corridor and into the cross passage. The door in which Benjie had showed such interest now stood ajar.

Hildy pushed it back so they could enter. 'How she get this open we never can learn. It is mystery.' She motioned through another door. 'Her bed is there. We put her in it, take off her shoes, and she never remember she was outside.

'A sore head is all she know, and she is used to that for she often bang it against the wall, thump, thump. When Andy stay in the room across the hall, he hear her many times.'

Marise paused, transfixed by the blaze of color covering the walls of the square sitting room through which she helped carry Penelope. But it was only later that she recalled in any detail the paintings that hung there. Now she could think only of getting the unfortunate woman into her bed.

Hildy turned the covers down as Andy heaved and Marise guided Penelope Clarrington onto her own bed. They stood back while Hildy removed the sneakers from her long, narrow feet and pulled the comforter up to her chin.

Lying there, eyes closed, face slack, she looked altogether too much like Ben as she had seen him so many times. The lines of maturity were smoothed from the oval face, and the dark hair spilled across her pillow. Marise reached to smooth the tangles into order. Those glossy tendrils even felt like Ben's.

'What a shame,' she said to the waiting couple. 'So much talent. And she's shut up here for all her life. I don't wonder she gets out whenever she can, but how in the world does she do it?'

There was no mark of prying or chipping on either side of the door. The bolts were undamaged, and Marise could only feel they had been shot from the outside, leaving the way clear for the prisoner to escape. The crossbar of the heavy lock was turned. Who could or would have done this?

'It is always so,' Hildy said. 'Never any sign to say how she has it opened, but no one here would dare to. Always, always for years it has been so, when she got out.'

'I've heard there are people who are geniuses when it comes to escaping,' Marise said. 'She has one kind of genius. Why not another? I wonder if she has some strange gift of that nature.' She sighed.

'However it is, we'd better put everything back as it was, for whatever that is worth. I'll talk to Ben about it when he comes in tonight.' She pushed the four bolts smoothly into their sockets and turned the handle of the lock.

'A long time ago,' she said, 'Benjie found his way up here. Father Clarrington heard him, and when I came after him he was at this door. You don't . . . suppose . . . he couldn't know who was inside.'

'No!' Hildy's high voice was emphatic. 'It has happened many times, long before you came and years before Benjie was born. How it happens I cannot say. Don't worry about this. We find some way, maybe, to keep her inside now.'

Ben went at once to the upper floor and checked the bolts on his sister's door.

She knew, for she went with him.

Heaven knew, they had tried. Ben installed a new lock that night, along with two more bolts, one let into the facing above the door, and he also screwed on hasps and padlocked the door. 'If that doesn't hold her, nothing will,' he said grimly.

Marise had reached for his hand, for she could see the pain in his eyes. Wordlessly, they locked their fingers together and stood staring at that enigmatic door.

'If we only knew how it's done,' Ben said. 'Even, mad though it would make them seem, the person or persons who might open it for her. Something! Anything to solve this.' He sounded defeated, and he had been. They never did solve the mystery of Penelope's escapes, try as they would.

Now Marise turned off the light and stared again around the dim shape of Hannibal's room. It was now bare of any trace of the hearty man who had lived in it. Even the memory of Penelope was growing dimmer, she found with some thankfulness.

Maybe time and increasing age would succeed at last in erasing the terrible years from her mind. As opposed to the possibility of her own madness, blank senility would be a blessed relief.

6

The Trustees were meeting in the board-room of Clarrington Enterprises. Evan Turner sat at the head of the polished table with Gertrude Fisk, head of their legal staff, at his right. Four other trustees were clumped nearby, leaving a long expanse of empty chairs.

Gertrude cleared her throat as Corrigan, the securities officer, completed his report. Evan could tell she was anxious to say something, for she kept shifting in her seat, giving the impression of nervous energy controlled with difficulty.

'If I might say something,' she said at last.

Corrigan relinquished the floor grace-fully. 'Of course.'

She leaned forward eagerly. 'I had occasion to speak with Mrs. Clarrington recently, when she called in her usual request for her grocery delivery. She asked also, at that time, for the balance sheets for every branch of the business. This seems to me to be both presumptuous on her part and a waste of time on ours

'It seems to me that her behavior has escalated enough to have her declared incompetent, removed from titular control of the estate, and assigned a guardian. Waiting on her signature or her approval for new projects has slowed business severely.

'This eccentric recluse cannot possibly comprehend either the balance sheets or the attendant reports. Her input is irrelevant and even, at times, disruptive. I think it is time we had her committed, either to an institution or to the care of some psychiatric nurse who could attend to her personal needs.'

Evan glanced at the faces of his associates, all of them young, now, except his own. Nobody but he had been a part of the firm at the time the Clarrington family had shrunk to a single widow, barricaded in her huge house.

He sighed and stood. 'I must make this extremely clear,' he said as the others shifted uneasily. 'Some of you already know some of the facts I will mention. It is doubtful if you can really comprehend the whole truth unless you listen hard.

'First, you have to understand that eccentricity is not insanity. No competent judge is going to rule that it is. Only if Mrs. Clarrington began neglecting her house and her person would I ever consent to consider such a procedure. None of this has happened or has shown signs of occurring.'

Ed Grebel, the accountant, raised his hand and Evan nodded toward him. 'You have to admit, Evan, it isn't normal for anyone to become a hermit. Not in this day and age, whatever used to happen in the distant past. No one sees the woman to know how or what she's doing or how she's getting along.'

'You're forgetting, Ed, *I* see her.' Turner kept his voice cool. 'I see her every month, without fail. I send Alistair with her groceries and other necessities. He always has tea with her in her parlor, after he puts things away for her. Never has he had anything but compliments for her personal appearance and the neatness of her house.

'We both marvel at how well she manages, all alone, to keep that huge place going. She is quite organized and orderly, and when I go we *do* discuss those balance sheets and reports. Thoroughly. She understands just what is going on in every segment of this business in which her competence lies. She keeps at me until I explain to her satisfaction all the rest that is not in her field of expertise.'

Gertrude frowned. 'Are you absolutely certain? Sometimes unbalanced people can be very persuasive.' She tapped her pencil on the table impatiently.

Evan shook his head. 'Don't forget that I have known her almost since she married Ben Clarrington, and I can bear witness that she managed the farms almost from the first days of her marriage. She was reared on a farm. Her understanding of agriculture is solid.

'She absorbed Ben's theories of silviculture, and she keeps a knowing eye on our practices in that area. Heaven forbid that she ever should catch you, Englund, clear-cutting. Considering the stability of our timber branch's profits, Ben's theories have been proven ten times over.'

Englund squirmed, and Evan knew the young man had envisioned huge machinery capable of clearing large tracts, then replanting with finger-sized trees. This was a good chance to drive home the company policy before he brought that subject up again.

'Marise Clarrington has a clear and logical mind. She understands bookkeeping; never doubt it. While she may remain inside her house and run things from there, that does not mean she doesn't know what we are doing and how we are doing it.'

Englund flushed. 'The big companies are making pots of money with clear-cutting. It saves time and labor, which both mean big money, and the row planting makes it possible to use machinery to harvest. I've begged and pleaded to be allowed to clear-cut, and you tell me this unstable woman is the reason we can't do it! I just can't accept that.'

'Then you'd better quit and go to work for one of the biggies,' Turner said pleasantly. 'Or one day I'll find a note in the mail asking me to replace you with someone who will hew to company policy. What you can't see past the dollar signs in your eyes is the fact that we have a constant, unvarying supply of saw timber and will have for the foreseeable future. When its price is high, we harvest hardwood. When that sinks we harvest pine.

'We do not own one single acre of bare land that will require fifteen or twenty years to produce a crop of inferior pine timber. No other outfit in this country, large or small, shows the profit margin that we do. Think that over and keep still.'

Turner saw a flicker of movement from Corrigan. Evan nodded in his direction.

The securities man said, 'That may be true. Nobody denies the company is solid as a rock, but there are things we could do — like short-term, high-interest investments — that could be extremely profitable, if we were allowed to take advantage of them. Any other enterprise this large would be forced to take such measures by the stockholders.'

Evan smiled. 'But there are no stockholders, as you know very well. The entire corporation is privately owned by Marise Clarrington, except for the small parcel Ben left me in his will.

'Each one of us is paid directly by Marise Clarrington, and every one of our jobs is at her disposal. Never forget that, and don't think I don't know why you are fidgeting to get Marise's hand off the controls, Gertrude.

'There is a lot of money and lot of power tied up in Clarrington Enterprises. Declaring the owner insane would open up the possibility of the firm going public. That would give every one of us an inside opportunity to buy hefty blocks of shares in a highly profitable company.

'If you think I don't see how your minds work, you are mistaken. I do. You are typical of those running business these days, and I understand you. Never think I don't know what you're up to.

'Any attempt to haul Marise Clarrington up on an insanity charge will find me squarely in her corner. I learned my trade the old-fashioned way, from honest and honorable people. I know you're not deliberately dishonest, any of you, but you are a generation removed from an inherent understanding of the concept of honor. Mind your manners, Trustees. I am watching you.'

There was no further discussion of the matter. The chastened group sat shuffling their reports back into their folders and filed out of the room. Evan stood for a long time afterward, staring down at his reflection in the polished wood.

He thought of Ben and Marise, of Hannibal and Emanuel. They were solid, dependable people. Not perfect, of course, but honest even in their imperfection. He was bound to them inextricably, and he could do no differently.

None of them, Marise, in particular, had deserved the fates marked out for them. She would not be thrown to the young and ambitious sharks if he could help it.

★　★　★

143

The thing that had taken place in Aunt Lina's room had been so incredibly vile that the very horror of it had helped Marise blank out the memory. It was something the mind could not retain without self-destructing. She found herself able to approach this room as a place where she had often found comfort, instead of terror.

The room still held a faint breath of sandalwood, for she had never disturbed Lina's old-fashioned furniture and her personal items, which were still arranged neatly on the dresser and the bedside table. Even her clothing still hung in the closet, for Marise had not been able to bring herself to go through Aunt Lina's things.

Always a haven of peace and sanity, this room, almost alone of those in the house, had resisted the residue of the mad thing that had happened here. The understanding and comfort Lina had dispensed to her nephews, and to Marise, seemed to override the later occurrence.

For Angelina Clarrington had been the pivot around which the family moved.

Unobtrusive, rather shy and plain, Lina was always there when she was needed, and she supplied whatever was required without fuss and with great kindness.

Benjie had found a special relationship with his great-aunt, and he had gone there often for a quiet talk with her.

Marise was glad of that, of course, for Lina had seemed at loose ends until Emanuel's illness made her feel useful again. She had taken willing turns at his bedside.

Standing there, remembering, Marise was relieved that she had insisted that the room be returned to its normal condition after it was cleaned up. Now it held an air of waiting. If only Lina could return, just for a brief time, to counsel with her!

Marise understood that anyone outside her peculiar situation might find this need of hers less than sane. Still she clung to the faint presence of Lina that remained in her chamber, lacking anything more concrete to comfort her.

The day after her encounter with Penelope, she had come here. Ben had needed all the comfort she could give, and she managed at last to convince him she had not suffered and he should feel no guilt. But her husband suffered from restless dreams that night, and she had not rested. When Ben left for the woods, she came down the half stair and tapped on Lina's door.

Aunt Lina had been crying, which was in itself so unusual as to be almost frightening. She had met Marise at the door, where she opened her arms and gathered the girl in like a lost lamb. For a moment she wept softly. Then she beckoned her into the room.

'This would happen on a day when I was away,' she sniffed. 'My dearest girl, I don't know what to say to you. We had no right at all to allow you to get into such a fix without any warning. We should have sent you and Ben away at once, before you settled in here. That first night when you came down to meet us, Emanuel should have told you the plain truth.' She wiped her eyes on a cambric handkerchief and regained control of herself.

'I should have told you myself, if he did not. My conscience has tortured me ever since, and it's been worse since Hanni died. How could we expect you, unwarned, unprotected, to deal with such a tragedy as ours?'

Marise drew Lina toward her small rosewood desk. 'Do sit down, Aunt Lina. And don't think it has all been terrible, for it hasn't. I've had a family, which I didn't have, after my brother died. I've been happy here, despite what has happened. This cannot dim it for me. Not ever.' She blinked back tears of her own.

'It's just that I was frightened yesterday. I never remember being that frightened before in all my life. Penelope's big and strong, and for a little while I was totally intimidated. Then I remembered my nurse's training and got my wits back. I didn't tell Ben I was afraid; he was too upset himself . . . '

'Well, I should think you would be afraid! You're such a little thing, I still don't know how you managed to knock her out. But thank God you did. The girl attacked me that way, years ago.

'She was hardly more than a child, and it was shortly after we had realized there was something wrong. It was after the . . . the event with the neighbor child, and we thought that if we could watch her closely enough we might still let her have just a bit of freedom.

'Emanuel hired a man to repair the iron fence around the gardens, for there were loose rods in places. Some of the mortar in the brick base was crumbling too. They put it into tiptop shape, so she could wander around the grounds without risk.

'She was playing around the rockery one day, and I was keeping an eye on her. She had her doll out there, with her tea set, and I thought she looked completely normal, pouring tea into the little cups and pretending the sort of tea table conversation children seem to think adults indulge in.

'It was late spring and warm, I remember. The roses smelled heavenly, and bees were buzzing around the jasmine. I was tired and I dozed off.' Aunt Lina closed her eyes for a moment, as if reliving that long ago instant of drowsiness.

Then her jade green eyes opened again, fixed upon the past.

'I don't know what waked me. She must have made some sort of sound when she picked up a discarded iron rod from the fence. You know those spears that form the tops of them? She ran at me full-tilt, the spear leveled toward my chest. She wasn't more than thirty feet away, but something lent me more wit and speed than I ever needed before.

'I'd been reading the leather-bound Shakespeare from the library. I raised it just in time, and the point of the spear went an inch and a half into the book before the resistance slowed her to a stop.'

Marise pictured the scene and shuddered. Blinking away the vision, she whispered, 'What on earth did you do?'

'I got up very carefully and pulled the spear out of the book. I smoothed out the puncture mark as well as I could, making regretful noises about damaging a book. Pen was staring at me as if she were disappointed, but I paid no heed to her. Once I got the book back into something like a readable condition, I said, 'Let's go ask Hildy for milk and cookies.'

'She took my hand and smiled as if nothing had happened, and we went away to the kitchen. I never told Emanuel. I never told anyone until now, though I watched my eyes out of their sockets after that. But now I am warning you. Never trust her, no matter what she says or how gentle she seems.'

Marise swallowed hard, her mouth suddenly dry. 'Didn't they consider . . . didn't they ever consider putting her someplace where she would be supervised by trained people?'

Lina looked at her hands. 'Yes, we did. We looked at all sorts of places, public and private, and Emanuel even talked about trying to establish one of his own, when he found out the conditions in even the best of the existing establishments. But that would have been very expensive, and it would have had to be staffed with the same kind of people who ran the others.

'There was no guarantee that Pen would be treated any better, or more competently than we could. And Ben wouldn't hear of it.

'He refused to agree to anything of the sort. He was still very young, of course, but there was never any shaking him once he made up his mind. He held it against all of us for years, the fact that we'd considered putting her away. She was his twin, no matter what.'

Lina looked up at Marise, her jade eyes opaque. 'I remember Ben shouting at his father, one night, 'We take care of our own!' when the subject of Penelope came up. 'Clarringtons caused this thing and Clarringtons must take care of it.'

'But after that he couldn't bear to stay here and see his sister become more and more troubled and unstable. For even after we found that if we supplied canvas and paint she was more settled, remaining quiet and contented for weeks at a time, she still broke out unexpectedly. It was clear her mind had not stopped deteriorating.' Lina rose stiffly from her desk and looked about the room absently.

'So Ben ran away and got sick and almost died and found you. Perhaps it would have been better for you, in the long run, if he hadn't . . . lived.'

'Don't ever say that!' Marise cried, flinching. 'Whatever happens, Ben has been worth everything. And Benjie and you and the rest of the family. I had nobody. I wasn't unhappy, but never on my best day did I claim to be happy. Nothing can take that away. I lived in a vacuum, and Ben came and filled my life.'

★   ★   ★

Marise, standing in the chilly room, remembered the warm conviction that had filled her as she spoke. She'd meant those words, totally and to the depths of her being. Indeed, she continued to mean them, up to the very end.

The room was quiet around her, the scent of sandalwood faint but pervasive. Marise touched the rosewood desk with one finger, wondering. If she had known then, would she have remained in this house? Would she have had the courage to stay here, anticipating the unseen but looming future?

No. For her son's sake, she would have

taken him and fled, if some vagrant intuition had told her what was beyond the horizon. She would have taken the family with her, if she could, but she knew without any doubt that they would never have left this place.

Ben wouldn't. Mother Clarrington couldn't. Aunt Lina would have felt bound here by years of dedication to her duty. Only Marise and Benjie could have managed to leave the cut granite house and close the iron spear gate behind them. Only they would have been safe.

In a way, she thought that might have been worse for her, but for Benjie she would have assumed even worse guilt than leaving the family to its fate. For Benjie she would have done terrible things, she knew.

But there had been no kind intuition, and now there were no more tears. Not for ten years had she possessed tears to spend. They had all been wept out long ago.

★　★　★

The man had long since learned her routine. He pretended, every morning, to leave for work, but he had found a spot in the vacant lot beside the Clarrington house from which he could see both the front and the rear gates. An untidy privet hedge that had run wild on the empty grounds formed a hole into which he could dive, remaining unseen but watchful as the days passed.

Although there was seldom any sign of life except a faint gleam from a crevice in the shutters of the tower rooms or a crack between draperies that shot a spear of light into the darkness of the gardens, he knew that life did go on there. An orderly, leisurely progression of events took place.

He'd ventured up in the light from the street lamp and seen the revolving mailbox that allowed her to take in her mail without opening her door. The mailman had a key to the front gate, and he opened it every morning to deposit the mail in its mouth-like slot.

The watcher marked that fact into his memory.

A middle-aged man arrived every

month, not on exactly the same day of the week or date but roughly at the same time of the month. Another, younger, man, brought boxes monthly as well. The boy accompanying him carried those around to the rear, while the man went up the steps, rang, and was admitted into the house.

This one visited at less regular intervals, sometimes once in the month, sometimes in only a couple of weeks. She must telephone when she needed something.

Nobody else approached the house, and only those three seemed to have keys to the forbidding front gate, as far as he could tell. He mulled over the fact for a very long time.

'There has to be some warning,' he muttered in his privet cover. 'It mustn't happen too quickly. She has to dread something terrible for a while. It isn't worth doing, unless it's done right.'

In time, he decided to write a note. Then he took a bus thirty miles to Duncanville, where he dropped it into a mailbox. That faithful mailman would deliver it, he knew, within a couple of days.

Then he would act. The thought made warm blood rush to his face and fill his chest with triumph.

He'd waited for a very long time now. He'd hated her for such a long while. But now she was about to pay. Soon. Soon.

★　★　★

Marise avoided the basement, for cleaning there seemed unnecessary and masochistic. But when a leaky faucet upstairs demanded a new washer, which in turn required a visit below to turn off the water, she knew she must go down into Hildy and Andy's empty domain. She hadn't visited it since that last dreadful day and had intended never to go there again.

To get to the main turnoff, she had to go through Hildy's sitting room. She approached the door with sick apprehension, though there could be nothing there now. Not after ten years. The door opened to a shower of loosened cobwebs, which was disgraceful.

Marise felt a twinge of conscience. She'd kept the upper floors clean, if not immaculately. She had been a coward when it came to this part of the house, and Hildy would have been distressed at the condition of her own quarters.

A small spider dropped onto her arm, and she brushed it off with distaste. She really must come down here with a broom to remove those webs. Perhaps a can of the spray that Alistair had brought her to combat ants and roaches might help. There was a scuttering sound in the corner, and small claws rasped against the cement floor. She added rat poison to her mental list.

The braided orange and brown rug was all but invisible beneath a thick layer of dust. Little puffs followed her steps across the floor as she moved into the room.

Hildy's crochet work huddled in a bright heap on the round table beside her cushioned chair. Andy's pipe lay where he had dropped it beside his own chair. Only the most necessary cleaning had been done after their deaths, and Marise hadn't been in the room then or since.

Evan Turner had suggested that she avoid it, and she had accepted his advice gratefully.

The last time she had been here was quite a while before the end of her world. She had taken down a prescription for Hildy, and when she tapped on the door Andy had grunted an invitation to come in.

The two of them had been sitting in their identical chintz-covered chairs, one on each side of the little table. An electric teapot was steaming on a trivet at the old cook's elbow.

The canary was singing loudly in its cage, and the scene would have presented a picture of domestic bliss, if it had not been for the reek of whiskey. Andy carried that about with him, wherever he went, like a second skin.

Hildy took one of the pills at once, washing it down with a cup of her freshly made tea. Marise had accepted a cup too, and they had sat in the warmth of the basement parlor, comfortably silent.

Marise had watched Hildy's round, fair face, noting a change as the medication took effect. The easing of pain lines in her forehead and about her mouth was obvious and immediate.

She'd nodded with satisfaction. 'I can see that one's probably going to work,' she said to Hildy. 'Is there any sign of sickness yet?'

Hildy breathed deeply, as if checking out her interior. 'Not yet, and the other pain medicine made me nauseated very soon. You think this will do, eh?'

'Well, the doctor said if this didn't do the job he'd have to go to something stronger, so I hope this one works,' Marise said.

Andy grunted, raising one bushy white eyebrow. Hildy, used to his wordless signals, nodded and said, 'Before you go, I need to say something. We think, Andy and I, all the time about how Pen could possibly have got out of her room. If nobody else do it, then she must do it herself. Maybe there is some way to make bolts move from inside the door, you think? Like with magnet?'

Marise remembered staring into her cup, her mind busy. 'Possibly. I don't know . . . aren't the bolts made of brass? But I'll ask Ben. He will know.' She frowned.

'Still, that would leave the lock, one of those heavy duty ones. I don't know how even a magnet could have opened that one, do you?'

Hildy sighed. 'Pen, she is clever with hands. Maybe she can make key? We do not know this, we just worry and think. Could a person make a key to fit such a lock out of something in her room? Maybe the little dull knife in her paint box?'

Marise had a sudden vision of a patient woman chipping away at a paint knife, shaping a key in blind hope that it would fit a lock she could not see and whose working parts she could not know.

'I have not seen that little knife in some time, when I clean her room,' Hildy continued. 'I worry. Andy also worry. Grown people can run or they can fight. But Benjie . . . what could he do against her?'

The echoes of that question followed Marise down the years into the present, as she stood on the dusty rug. She could still hear Hildy's shrill voice speaking the words and Ben's deep voice exploring the possibilities as he thought about it.

It had already been too late, though they hadn't known it. They had done their pointless talking, their useless searching of Penelope's room. Things had gone too far to stop, although nothing at the time had warned them of the fact.

Marise moved across the room and into the pantry-like cubby where the water cutoff waited. She twisted the lever over, hurried out of the dusty space, and sped back to the door. Once there she turned and looked back. She avoided looking at the scrubbed spot, which was still paler than the rug, though its outlines were softened by the layering of dust.

'I'm sorry, Hildy,' she whispered. 'So sorry.'

Then she hurried up the steps to the ground floor and closed the door at the head of the stair. She felt better with it solidly shut against the thing that had happened below.

Whenever she passed the door of Mother Clarrington's room, Marise always thought of Edenson. The nurse had been so jealous of her domain that Marise felt awkward whenever she went there. Yet her presence seemed to comfort her mother-in-law so much it was worthwhile putting Miss Edenson's nose out of joint. She was, after all, employed to care for her patient, not to supervise her list of visitors.

Yet now Marise felt Edenson's presence even more than she did that of her mother-in-law. Though the woman had not been obtrusive, Marise had always known she was sitting quietly in her chair beyond the screen or lurking in her adjoining bedroom.

You would have thought she felt they were conspiring to get rid of her. Or had she thought Marise might harm her patient? That was an uncomfortable notion.

She brought Benjie, if possible, when she visited Mother Clarrington, and the older woman seemed to be stimulated and pleased. The boy never seemed to know what to make of his grandmother, for illness had not yet forced its way into his young world. The concept of pain was one she had a hard time getting across to him.

'I know how I look,' the old woman said sadly to Marise, once. 'Like the living dead, in fact. I wouldn't want to be kissed by these cold blue lips, and I know someone as full of life as Benjie doesn't like to either.' She sighed and closed her eyes.

When she opened them, their pale gaze was fixed on Marise's face. 'I have missed it all, child. I wasn't able to mother my own children, after Hannibal. My wretched heart laid me low after . . . after the twins. My sister-in-law got to kiss all the skinned knees. She got the rambunctious hugs and helped to catch the runaway kittens.' She drew a tearful breath.

'She got to do all the things I'd have given my soul to do. I was grateful to have her help, but I envied her too. Lina has been closer, dearer than my own sister would have been, if she'd lived. Though we had a few spats when I was a young bride, they were never serious.

'Her strength has kept me going when my own was exhausted, and now Emanuel is gone, you and Ben and Lina hold me to life. I know I'm unnecessary, but not one of you has ever hinted at that. I'm grateful for it.' She moved restlessly against her pillows.

Edenson appeared as if by magic, touching the thin wrist, examining the pale face with anxious eyes. 'You must not tire her!' she whispered venomously.

'She will tell me when she's tired,' Marise replied, keeping her composure. 'It isn't good for her to lie here for days seeing only you, Miss Edenson. She needs stimulus, even if it's only the mild kind I can supply.'

Edenson glared. Then, without another word, she went into her own room and closed the door. Though it shut with a faint click, the effect was that of a slam. Marise knew that, with the best will in the world, she had angered Edenson yet again.

'Has Benjie gone outside?' her mother-in-law asked.

Marise nodded. 'He heard Ben come

home, I think. The two of them are inseparable when they have the chance. It'd do your heart good to see them packing up fishing gear to go to the lake. They've been planning this trip for a month.' She leaned forward and smiled.

'For men only, of course. It has been made quite clear to me several times, in the kindest possible terms. You wouldn't think a ten-year-old would have that much tact, would you?'

Mrs. Clarrington relaxed and smiled back at her. 'He's a bright, loving little boy. Though I see him so little, I can feel it in him. You won't mind, I hope, if I say I was very much relieved when we could be certain the family taint had not touched him. Having children is such a gamble.' For a moment she looked infinitely sad.

'We lost that gamble, Emanuel and I, in one out of our three. Believe me, Marise, there is nothing on earth more painful than realizing your own child is defective. Dangerous, even. When Emanuel told me about the Clarrington flaw, I was sure my own sturdy ancestors would outweigh that unfortunate inbreeding, which, after all, is many generations removed by now. I was cocksure, as young people tend to be!' She gave a bitter laugh, and Marise reached to take her cold hand between her own warm ones.

Elizabeth said, 'I know you must have wondered why we went ahead and had children, after poor little Clara. But my own certainty was a large part of the reason. The other was that we were so deeply in love I felt sure it would make no difference anyway.' She shivered slightly, her hand quivering in Marise's.

'I will admit I was nervous while I carried Hannibal. It would have required a woman made of stone not to be, after the horror stories I'd heard. But Hanni was a merry little guy, from the day he was born. He was the steadiest, most reasonable child I ever knew. Even in his cradle, you could talk to him, explain things to him, and he understood, though nobody believed me when I told them.'

'He was always that way when I knew him,' Marise agreed. 'Right up to the day he died I felt him as a solid reassurance in the family. I've always thought he must have been the sort of baby Benjie was, busy with his own thoughts and projects, open to new interests, but not at all demanding.'

'Exactly. The entire family was so delighted with Hanni; even Emanuel's father seemed to come alive again, for a time, for he'd been like a man lost in a nightmare since the night when his wife and daughter died. His joy in Hanni was a lovely thing to see, for he almost went into shock when Emanuel told him we would have a child.

'The thought that another generation might have to deal with the tragedies he'd known made him frantic. Hanni changed that and gave us the courage to try again.' She moved her hand restlessly, and Marise released it.

'If only we'd been content with what we had!' Elizabeth was silent for a long moment. Then she shook her head. 'But hindsight does no one any good. The twins came, beautiful and bright like their brother. It was obvious from their first day of life that each was a unique person, though Ben reminded us of Hanni. More demanding, of course, but that was natural. We spoiled both of the babies badly, and Hanni was more indulgent with them than any of us adults. He couldn't bear for either of them to cry.'

'What about Penelope?' Marise had wondered what sort of child she had been.

'She was different, but because I had never had a girl I thought it was just the gender that made the difference. Much of it may have been, too. She was beautiful, talked a month before Ben, and was walking when he was still scooting along on his bottom.

'When she was three she began to draw these marvelous pictures. I saved many of them because they were imaginative and very well done for so young a child. Yet before she was five I became strangely uneasy about her.'

Marise leaned forward, reaching for an answer. 'Why?'

'I could see something behind her eyes. There was something about her reactions to other people as well. As quietly as I could, I warned Lina to watch her closely, though I think I didn't make it forceful enough. Perhaps if I had managed that, the child next door might have been spared . . . '

Marise smoothed the coverlet into place. 'We can't dwell on what might have been,' she said. 'Ben told me enough of it. I can't blame you in the least for being uneasy about Benjie. I have to admit I wondered too.' She rose briskly.

'Now I must go, for the farm waits. And you are getting tired. I can see that. I'll come in tomorrow for a few minutes.'

There had been many tomorrows, for every morning she would visit Mother Clarrington with news of the family and the business, of her grandson and her son. Though Ben went up every evening, he was never good at conveying such trivia, his mother complained to Marise.

'You make me see what is happening,' she said. 'Ben just hands me a string of words. He's a dear boy, but he doesn't tell a story nearly as well as you do.'

That pleased Marise, for she was very fond of her mother-in-law and valued her friendship. Every day she looked forward to their quiet half hour, though at times she carried away disturbing information.

One morning Mother Clarrington met her with an unwelcome notion. 'You know, some nights Penelope comes to my room,' she said. 'She came last night and talked to me in the dark. She said terrible things, but she always does. They seem real to her, I think, although they're not.'

Marise felt cold along her bones. She and Ben had felt so certain the new locks and bolts would stop Penelope's prowling about the house.

'Are you sure you're not dreaming?' she asked. 'That new medication can make you have mild hallucinations.' Though she asked the question, she felt uneasily that she was wrong.

Mother Clarrington shook her head. 'I've been sedated and medicated for too many years to mistake hallucination for reality. I know the difference. No, it was Pen. She never comes very close to me, but I can tell she hates me. I can hear it in her voice, as well as in her words.' She reached to grasp Marise's hand with desperate strength.

'Ben must check everything carefully, once again. Pen is so full of hate. She told me . . . she said she frightened Hannibal to death with something she said, though I find that hard to believe. He knew her too well, and even if he hadn't expected to find her there in the library, that by itself would never have shocked him enough to kill him. I am certain of that.'

Again she squeezed Marise's fingers. 'Have Ben check.' Her voice failed, and only her pale eyes pleaded.

So they redoubled their efforts, changing locks and bolts. They warned Benjie seriously against even going down the third floor corridor, and he accepted the warning, wide-eyed but cooperative.

Nevertheless, when Marise was waked from a sound sleep one night, weeks later, the door on the third floor was the first thing that came to mind. The rapping on her sitting room door had brought her upright, dreading what she might find.

Ben was already on his feet, one arm in a sleeve of his robe, his feet shuffling for his slippers. 'I'm coming,' He called. 'Just a minute.'

A muffled voice was babbling indecipherable words from the half landing outside their door as the two hurried down their short flight of steps. Edenson stood in the dim pink light from the tulip lamps, her hair mussed, her eyes filled with tears.

'It's your mother. She . . . was dead when I went in to give her the three o'clock medications.' Those flinty eyes were softer than Marise had ever seen them, the sure hands unsteady.

She realized suddenly that this homely and unloved little woman had been genuinely fond of her patient and was grief-stricken now she was dead. Perhaps that was the only emotional connection in the nurse's life, Marise thought, as she tied her robe firmly around her waist.

'We'll go with you right now. Ben, please call Aunt Lina while I go with Miss Edenson. Come, my dear.' She saw the woman was shaking, her teeth almost chattering. 'You're cold,' she said. 'Let me get my sweater off the couch. Now . . . better? Let's go up together.'

She took the nurse's hand and held it

tightly as they hurried to the second floor. Edenson did not object to having her hand held until they neared the door of the hospital suite. Then she tugged it loose, smoothed down her hair with a nervous gesture, and sank back, to some extent, into her professional mold.

'I can manage now,' she said, her voice steady and cold again. Her gaze flickered aside, then back to Marise. 'Why don't you . . . go up and see if your husband needs help.'

Marise nodded. 'I'll peep into Benjie's room as I go back. I don't want him disturbed. It won't take long, but do call the doctor.'

'I did that at once,' Edenson said, offended.

'Of course you did. Listen for the bell and let him in when he comes, will you? Andy doesn't wake easily, and we may be out of hearing.'

She turned and flew up to the third floor, knowing Ben would have gone there, after waking his aunt. The corridor was dimly lit, for Ben had switched on the flower basket fixtures. She could see him as she turned the last corner, bent over the locks on that door.

'It was closed? Locked?' she panted.

'Tight as possible. She hasn't been out tonight, I can guarantee that. Poor Pen. Why did we immediately suspect she might have caused mother's death, after all these years of expecting her heart to give out at any time? But it was the first thing that came to mind.' He fingered the middle bolt.

'Should we tell her?' he asked.

Marise sighed. 'Not until tomorrow anyway. Come down now, dearest. We have to see the doctor and tell Hildy and Andy. How is Aunt Lina?'

'I tapped on her door and told her before she got there. Then I headed up here. I felt in my bones that I'd find the door wide open and Pen on the prowl. Thank God I didn't. This should be one Clarrington death that holds no shadow of doubt.'

When they got back to the hospital suite they found the doctor there with Edenson. Aunt Lina stood like a pillar of fire in her red robe, her jade green eyes wet. But she controlled her tears, as she seemed able to control most of her reactions, no matter how distressing the situation.

She opened her arms, and Ben went into them as if he were still the small boy she had reared. She patted his shoulder, smiling past it at Marise. That was a watery smile, but a brave one. Marise tried hard to return it.

The three waited in the corridor while the doctor and Miss Edenson remained closeted in the hospital suite. When the door opened at last, Doctor Pell stepped out, looked back, and closed it behind him.

Pell looked around at them, wiping his glasses absently with an immaculate handkerchief, despite the odd hour. He was a crumpled, gray little man, almost as familiar to Marise now as were the members of the family. Now he sighed.

'It has come, just as we expected for so many years. Evidently, she had an attack some time between midnight and three o'clock. Her death was quick and easy, as I expected. Miss Edenson said she seemed to feel fairly well at supper time, and it is obvious there was no illness and not even much pain. It was the end she hoped for, when the time came.

'You're lucky, Ben. These past years have been relatively easy for her, compared with those when you were a boy. You've had her a lot longer than I ever would have dreamed back then.'

She took his arm. 'Come downstairs, Dr. Pell. I'll make coffee. I know you need it, and the rest of us could use the warmth and the stimulation. I'll run ahead of you, if you don't mind, for Hildy would never forgive me if I didn't call her too. When Miss Edenson is ready, all of you come to the kitchen. We need something to steady us down.'

She remembered that as a night of grief and cold. She had felt lightheaded from lack of sleep, but she had known no deeper worry, as she had with the deaths of Hanni and Father Clarrington. She had not seen Mother Clarrington lying dead in her room.

No, the hospital suite had another dimension, for she had gone there to help

Edenson list the medications and box them for burning. Now that Edenson had no further reason to fear her as a rival, she found both of them, as nurses, had a horror of strong prescriptions left unattended in a house where a small child lived.

While they were in the suite, they sorted through Elizabeth Clarrington's personal possessions. They took her robes and nightgowns from bureau and closet, packing them into boxes to give to charity. For the first time since they met, Marise felt a closeness to the stocky little nurse. Her hostility seemed to have evaporated.

While she was taping the last box tightly, Edenson holding it together, Marise looked up to find the nurse's gaze fixed on her. 'Someone was in the room the night Mrs. Clarrington died,' Edenson said abruptly. 'I heard someone talking, through my sleep. I almost woke up, but I didn't quite make it fully awake.'

She looked sheepish. 'It's been hard for me to wake, these past few years. I had to set the alarm to get me up to give the meds. But I didn't dream this. I know as surely as I stand here that someone was in her room last night, talking.

'I heard her say, 'No! No!' I recall that perfectly clearly, and I struggled to get up and see what was happening, but I couldn't rouse myself enough. Later, when the clock woke me fully, I remembered at once as I went into the room.

'But there was no sign of anything wrong, and Dr. Pell said the death was natural. I didn't mention it to him, because there seemed no need to. With Penelope locked up, who could have been there? He'd have said I was dreaming.'

Marise looked down at the box, cutting the tape. She set the roll aside and turned to the little nurse. 'Perhaps Aunt Lina went in to check on her and found her awake. Lina told me she does that sometimes, when she can't sleep. Mother Clarrington slept very badly, as you probably know all too well, and they used to talk, sometimes, in the night.'

'I know that,' Edenson said. 'But it didn't sound like her voice. Yet I suppose it must have been . . . there's nobody else, is there?' Her voice wasn't nearly as assured as the words she spoke.

For some reason, Marise had never asked Aunt Lina if she had been that late night visitor to Mother Clarrington, and Lina had never said anything about going there that night. If she had been the one, everything was fine. If not . . . Marise didn't want to know it.

For Edenson was right. There was nobody else, or if there had been, it was someone whose existence Marise did not suspect. She wanted to keep it so, if possible.

Now she looked around the room, bare, sterile. The hospital bed was given to charity, too, along with the wheelchair.

The Matisse Mother Clarrington had loved so much had been placed in Marise's own sitting room. Only the bureau and the dressing table stood against the wall, bare and forlorn looking.

Marise sighed. There was no need to clean here. Nobody needed the space. She decided she would lock that room permanently. She didn't need the memories it held or the question that was raised there and had never been answered.

In the decade since her death, Marise had felt guilty about her relationship with Edenson. From the first she had allowed the nurse's defensive attitude to hold her at arm's length, and the thought still bothered her.

After all, she had possessed everything any woman could want. She was young and strong, well loved, if not beautiful, and she was busy with an absorbing profession, in addition to her husband and son. At the time Edenson had seemed simply a part of the furnishings, and once the woman made it clear she wanted no personal relationship with Marise she had left it at that.

Yet even before Elizabeth Clarrington's death, Marise had begun feeling somewhat unhappy about her relationship with the other nurse who had only her patient to fill her days. Edenson had worked faithfully for twenty years, putting everything she had into her patient's comfort and well-being.

Marise had worked with many nurses

in her professional career in medicine, and she knew that others would never consent to work seven days a week, without even a day off for themselves. They had lives of their own, and the fact that Edenson never consented to take a single day's holiday from her duties betrayed her lack of family and friends outside the Clarrington house.

That had made Marise a bit uneasy. So much so she once took it up with Dr. Pell. 'I know she is completely dedicated, Doctor, but this seems unhealthy to me. It is like something you find in an English novel — the devoted Nanny syndrome. Such selfless service doesn't exist in the world we know now. No nurse I ever knew, including myself, could or would have given up any semblance of a personal life in this way.'

The gray little doctor, a bit mussed as usual, had turned those alert eyes on her. He smiled rather sadly and said, 'I've thought that myself, to tell the truth. But Edenson's is a most unusual situation, and her relationship with Mrs. Clarrington is not the normal nurse-patient one.'

He leaned against the table in the library, where she had caught him after a conference with Father Clarrington, and said, 'I have known Edenson all her life. Her mother, Hester, went to school with Elizabeth and me. She was no beauty, but she was a highly determined young woman.

'She was unpopular in school. Single, focused young women tend to frighten young men away. Her people were farmers, well fed but without much money. However, she intended to make something of herself or die in the attempt. She worked her way through nursing school and became a damn good nurse.'

He looked about, found a chair and sat at the long library table. 'Here, sit down, for this is a long tale.'

Marise perched across the table and waited, and he went on, 'She was so good that when she went to New York she became a charge nurse at Bellevue. You know how much grit and ability that must have taken.

'She never intended to marry, which she made perfectly clear to everyone who knew her as a young woman. Yet when she was twenty-seven she met Arthur Edenson and married him. I never met Arthur, for he was killed three years after their marriage, and they had never come back here to visit. The wreck that killed him crippled Hester and injured their daughter, Edith, our Miss Edenson.'

'So Hester brought her daughter and came home again at last,' Marise observed. 'A natural thing to do, I should think.'

'Exactly. Though her parents were dead by then, they left their farm to her. She leased out the land at that time, but she left the house empty for some reason, though several people wanted to rent it. But it turned out for the best, for when they returned she had someplace to live without paying rent.

'She came back determined to be as independent as possible. The rent on the farm brought in a certain amount, mighty little, I can tell you, for it was hard times then for farmers. But the man who worked the place knew what he was about, and he supplied them with all the vegetables they could eat; Hester kept chickens and a couple of pigs, so they didn't go hungry.'

He stared down at the polished wood of the table and idly rubbed it with a forefinger. 'As long as Edith was small they didn't need much. Hester was well enough at times to take special nursing cases for me too. By that time I was established well enough in my practice to throw a good many cases her way, when she was able to handle them.

'But Edith wanted to be a nurse too. I managed to help her get a scholarship to a good school, but it provided only tuition and books. She needed more than that to make it, for the work was too hard to allow outside jobs for living expenses. I went to Elizabeth, who was always generous and who had liked and respected Hester. She gladly made up the lack for the child of her old schoolmate.

'Edith, being just as proud and independent as her mother, felt it as an obligation, though we both tried to convince her that the opportunity to help her made Elizabeth very happy.'

The doctor scratched his ear absently, his expression withdrawn. 'So Edith Edenson finished her course and got a degree afterward, a B.S. in nursing. She went to work in a big hospital in Charlottesville, and kept on with her education. She took a special degree in psychiatric nursing, and that helped her make enough to pay back every cent the Clarringtons had put into her education.

'She donated a scholarship to the nursing school that had provided her scholarship in the beginning. The girl saved like a miser, otherwise, never had any fun, and looked likely to become a psychiatric case herself, once her mother was gone.

'Then the twins were born and Elizabeth needed a nurse about as badly as anyone I ever knew. Edenson dropped her own career like a shot and came to care for her. Once we knew, without any doubt, that poor little Pen was mentally disturbed, she did the best she could to help deal with her too, for she knew a lot about mental illness. But nothing she tried seemed to penetrate the child's mind.

'Penelope was a lost cause, and we all knew it by that time. She needed close watching, if not institutionalizing. Her mother needed even more care than before, for her condition was deteriorating badly at the time. You might not believe it, but she has been relatively well the past few years, compared to what went before.

'Edith was invaluable. She shut away her past. I wondered if there had been an unhappy love affair to make her shut it off so completely, and devoted herself to making life bearable for Elizabeth. I agree with you. It isn't healthy. But when you know Edith's story, perhaps for her it is about as healthy as she can get.'

He sighed and rose. 'I don't know what happened to her as a girl, but I do know fear when I see it. That is what I see in her eyes every time I mention her going about finding a life of her own.'

After that, Marise left Edenson to her own devices. She'd been as friendly as the nurse would allow her to be, but she never really pushed it further than that. Then after Mother Clarrington died, when the two of them were in her room packing up her things, Marise found the chink in Edenson's armor for which she had waited so long.

'I talked with Ben last night,' she'd said to the nurse. 'You've been a part of this family for so long we can't get by without you. You probably have plans of your own, but if they're not pressing, would you consider staying on? At least for a while?' She studiously avoided looking at Edenson, concentrating on folding a set of underwear neatly.

'I am beginning to need someone to look out for Benjie, now that he's old enough to go to school functions and baseball games, and the farm keeps me hopping. And then there's Penelope. We never know when we'll need help with her. Aunt Lina hasn't been too well either. We do need you, you know.' She tucked the neat bundle into the box for Good Will.

Those flinty eyes had surveyed her sharply. But Edenson's mouth had actually curved slightly as she said, 'I haven't made any firm plans yet. I've known this had to happen for a long while now, but somehow I never really expected it would come so soon.' She put her own folded pile into the box, keeping her face turned away now.

'I really haven't anything much to do now Mother's gone. The farm gets along fine, and my renter is buying the place on installments, anyway. I still own the house, but it's old and needs a lot of repair before I could live in it.' There was the faintest suspicion of a sniff.

'I don't seem to make friends. I never did know why. Maybe it's because I'm . . . shy.'

Then she turned and attempted a real smile. 'I'll stay if you want me to. At least for the time being. We can see how things turn out, and I can always try to get another nursing position if it comes to that. It seems a shame to waste all my training. But you ought to know I'm not as strong as I was. Thank you.'

Marise had felt a surge of triumph. 'Then it's settled. At least for now.' She was relieved, for she had felt they would be turning out a waif into the world. In her own sphere, Edenson was a tower of strength. Elsewhere, Marise felt she was terribly vulnerable.

★ ★ ★

Marise shivered in the chill of the corridor before opening Edenson's old room. If she were to close off this suite, she should check the rooms for damp and mice. Then she could lock both doors and forget they existed. For Edenson's was another door she hated to open.

She had felt certain she had convinced the woman that they needed and wanted her. In the weeks following Mother Clarrington's death there had been work for everyone, and Edenson had proven her worth many times over.

That allowed Marise to go back to running the farms with her full attention, for she knew that Benjie would be supervised well when he was out of school. Otherwise, Edenson took over the surveillance and management of Penelope, to Andy's vocal relief. All in all, the diminished household ran smoothly and well.

It had been this, perhaps, more than anything else that made the ensuing shock even greater. One Sunday morning Edenson was late for breakfast. It had never happened before, and the family ate while wondering whether she might be ill. But she had been working so hard and seemed so weary that Marise decided to let her sleep for a while.

She hadn't appeared by noon, however, and Marise was shaken. She prepared a tray with tea and toast and took it upstairs. She tapped at the door, but there was no answer. No sound could be heard, though everyone in the family knew Edenson snored like a bear.

Marise remembered sorting through the keys to find the one that fitted this door. She opened it and knew at once the familiar odor that greeted her. She set down the tray and approached the bed to look down at what remained of Edith Edenson, R.N.

The nurse looked quite peaceful, seeming to sleep, for her eyes were closed. Beside the bed on the night stand there was an open packet, empty. Her nightly glass of milk had been drained, but she had not rinsed it in the bathroom adjoining her room, as she usually had done. A film of milk still coated the glass.

Marise touched nothing, though she leaned close to inspect the packet. Her heart began to thud sickly, for she recognized the container. The two of them had disposed of all the drugs left over from Elizabeth Clarrington's long illness, and they had done it together, bearing witness for each other. Yet this was one of the prescription sleeping drugs that should have been destroyed.

Had Edenson managed to secrete it before they went through the rooms? It would have been easy enough, Marise knew. Evidently she had done just that and at last had used the medication.

Had it been a sudden fit of depression? She had seemed quite cheerful in the past weeks, or at least as cheerful as her morose disposition would allow. Marise found herself puzzled, despite the obvious conclusion to be drawn at the pitiful bedside.

Dr. Pell came at once, and they stood

on either side of the bed, looking down at the slight shape beneath the covers. 'Did she have any physical problems?' Marise had asked the doctor. 'She had seemed very sleepy for a long while. She complained once that it took the alarm going off to wake her to give medications in the night.' She thought back, wondering if she had missed some important sign or symptom.

'She didn't look quite well these past weeks, but I felt certain she was grieving for Mother Clarrington. I caught her crying once, in the library. But other than that?'

'She was anemic. Came to see me before Elizabeth died,' the doctor said. 'I gave her a tonic for it. She certainly didn't need sleeping medicine. She told me the same thing. Said she could hardly keep awake sometimes. She found it hard to rouse herself in the mornings, and she said she fell asleep when she was still for more than just a moment or two.

'As far as I can tell, however, she had no serious health problem.' He glanced up and their eyes met. 'I think she just couldn't take it. Elizabeth was her life for so long that it left too large a gap in her existence. She must have kept this back; it's what I prescribed for Elizabeth's really bad nights. Three would have done the job, but she took the entire packet. She never knew what hit her. Poor girl!' He drew the sheet over the peaceful face.

'It's still an unattended death.' Marise said. 'What about all the official matters?'

'Oh, the coroner will want a statement from all of us, particularly you and me. They may want an autopsy, though I am altogether certain this is a suicide. But that's the procedure, quite often in cases of this kind. I'll call the authorities for you, but I don't know about funeral arrangements. Edith had no other kin, I think.'

Marise had shaken her head. 'Don't worry about that. She's been a member of this family for twenty years, and we'll see to everything when all is settled. If Ben agrees, and Aunt Lina too, I think we should put her on the other side of Mother Clarrington. I think they'd both have liked that.'

* * *

Now Edenson lay beside her longtime friend and patient. Not once in the ten years since she was put there had Marise visited their graves, though she had a standing order that flowers be put into the marble vase regularly and the Trust provided for perpetual care for the plot. It was the least she could do for the strange little woman who had consistently refused to be her friend.

Once inside that room, Marise paused to look around. The place was tidy, though very dusty. There was no point in cleaning it now, for there was no smell of mildew or mice. She sighed and turned her back on the chamber where Edith Edenson had lived for two decades.

There are many things I could and should have done, Marise thought. If I had been alert and taken everything into account, watched for warnings and indications, perhaps I might have saved those I love from what came afterward.

She closed the door behind her with a definitive click and turned the key in the lock that had not kept death away from the tenant of the room.

Another thought, which had haunted Marise for a decade and forced her to shut herself into this house, she pushed resolutely out of her consciousness. Yet it still lurked there, hard and cold as a pearl in an oyster.

What if it was I, all the while? What if I, all unknowingly, insanely, managed to help to do what was done to my family?

She had been left with that, at the end, for it could not have been Penelope, unaided, who brought things to their hideous conclusion.

7

Evan surveyed the front of the Clarrington house with a critical eye. It had always been his intention to keep the place up to the standard required by the family, and he felt he had done well, with Marise's help.

The ironwork was solid when he shook one of the iron spears. The shrubbery had been trimmed recently and looked crisp and tidy. The woodwork around the windows had been freshly painted and the stone façade had been cleaned. He was satisfied with the results of his efforts.

As he turned his key in the expensive lock securing the gate, he had a notion of movement beyond the tall privet hedge that divided the Clarrington grounds from the vacant lot beyond. He stared keenly through the bushes, but there was no repetition of whatever it was that had caught his eye. Perhaps a bird had hopped from branch to branch.

He shook the fence again, after locking the gate behind him. Nobody could possibly get into the grounds without a great deal of work and noise and a lot of trouble. The alarm system would betray any effort to get over or through the fence, except for this gate, and trying to jimmy the lock would set off its own alarm.

As well as possible, he had tried to protect Marise Clarrington from anyone who thought to find easy pickings in a widow living alone in such a huge house. He thought of Ben with grief, but he had begun thinking of Ben's widow in a more tender and personal manner. It had, after all, been ten years.

He rang the bell and waited for the click of her heels on the floor beyond the heavy door. After a moment the door opened, and her face, pale for lack of sun, beamed out at him.

'Evan! It is always so good to see you. Do come in.' She took his hat and hung it on the ornate hall tree with the mirror. He envied her that piece every time he saw it. But he followed her into the parlor, which was, as always, immaculate.

'I have coffee ready,' she said. 'You always come promptly at four o'clock on the dot. And I've just made a batch of Hildy's special cookies. Sit down. I'll be right back.' She tapped away down the hall, leaving him to check out her housekeeping without being obvious about it.

He sat in one of the deep chairs, looking about him. He thought of Gertrude's impassioned argument at the last meeting of the Trustees, and again he felt a flush of anger. He had never seen a room less likely to harbor someone who was unbalanced or incompetent.

Though it was tidy, it was not obsessively so. Marise had been reading, for her book lay face down on a small table beside her special chair. The print of her heels marked the upholstered otto-man. He peered at the book's title.

Thoreau. He smiled, for that was so like her. If she could not visit the woods in person, then she would go in spirit.

He heard her step in the corridor, and she was there with the tray. When they were settled with thin Belleek coffee cups in their hands and cookies within easy reach, he said, his tone serious, 'I've brought something besides balance sheets this time, Marise.'

She looked up, surprised. 'What on earth are you talking about?'

He sipped his coffee and set the empty cup on the piecrust table beside him. 'The natives are beginning to get restless,' he said, trying to lighten his own mood. 'Clarrington is a rich outfit, and the board members are looking at their own departments with ambition.

'There's too much money involved in the enterprises, and that can arouse greed in even the most dependable people. There've been rumbles of discontent from time to time. At the last meeting one of them actually suggested that you should be declared incompetent and given a guardian, taking control of the corporation away from you.' He felt sick at having to say the words, but her calm expression did not waver.

'I tried to make my position quite clear. But even if I succeeded, I'm afraid it will only be temporary. They have their eyes on you, and they are typical young materialists, without any understanding of people whatever.'

He leaned forward, hands on knees. 'You really ought to open up the house. Or better yet, sell this white elephant — or make a home for the elderly out of it. Come back into the world. Sit at the head of the table and give the orders you have been giving to me. Show them who you are.

'If anything should happen to me, they'd be at your throat. I have no doubt of that at all. They may even try to sidestep me now, keeping me in the dark until it's too late. You need to protect yourself. Besides,' — he tried to relax and be persuasive — 'it isn't right for someone to imprison herself this way. You lost all you loved, I know. But it shouldn't prevent you from living again.'

Her fair head tilted, the narrow face sober and the blue eyes intent while she listened. 'They have logic on their side,' she said. 'I can see their viewpoint, even if you can't. They're young and full of vigor.' Steel came into the line of her jaw.

'But this company doesn't belong to them. It boils down to that, doesn't it? Clarringtons worked and connived for generations to accumulate the elements of the enterprises, and this was not done in order to provide a bunch of upwardly mobile executives a quick way to wealth.'

Her eyes were bright and steady. 'This was left to me to run, for the good of the estate and its employees. I have to do that, like it or not. If Benjie . . . but I won't even bring that up.' He could see her swallow hard.

'I have never entirely confided in you, Evan, because I dislike even thinking about the thing I have to tell you. I actually can't bring myself to believe in it myself, and if I ever do bring myself to, I'll ask you to draft the papers allowing me to commit myself to a mental home. Yet this is a very real possibility I cannot discount.' She drew a deep breath, held it for a moment, and exhaled wearily.

'The last months before the tragedy were disturbing, stressful, and full of tension. Something in the very atmosphere of this house seemed threatening, menacing. It affected me very strongly. So much so that I found myself listening to sounds that I knew could not be there. Benjie's ball bouncing down the stair or Ben's voice heard unexpectedly in the hall could make me jump out of my skin.

'I lost weight and began to have trouble sleeping. Dr. Pell gave me tranquilizers, and they helped a bit. Not enough.

'I have thought about this for years now, and I believe they affected me in an unusual fashion. I would lose entire blocks of time, during which things would get done in the kitchen or about the house or out on the farms, but I couldn't recall doing them. Looking back, I find the thought terrifying.' And she looked frightened now, Evan thought.

'I believe I may have been at least partially responsible for what happened in this house that last evening. For this reason, I can't risk going out among others who might be harmed if I am actually mad. If I should be dangerous, let it be only to myself.'

He was suddenly angry. Not at her, but

at the maelstrom of madness and murder that had pulled her into its current, and, even now, would not let her go.

'That's insane!' he said.

She smiled. 'That is exactly what I fear,' she said.

'No, I don't mean you. Anyone who is actually insane never admits or suspects it. As a nurse, you should know that.'

'I also know there are as many exceptions to rules as there are rules,' she replied.

He tried another tack. 'But it was Penelope. The authorities were entirely satisfied that was the truth of the matter. They never questioned it.'

'I agree that Penelope did the deeds herself, with her demented brain and busy hands. Mostly. But there were aspects nobody ever examined. I have mulled this over for ten years, and I am left with a final, impenetrable fact. I was the only person left alive in the house. The only one who could possibly have let her out, and that allowed her to do . . . what she did.' She fought for control, and he saw her fingers clench in her lap.

'I don't remember doing it, but this isn't proof I didn't. God knows, before that evening ended I was more than half out of my mind, at best. At worst . . . I don't want to think about that, but I must. I have been thinking about it for ten years.'

Evan put the remnant of a cookie carefully onto the saucer. 'Marise, I have known you for a very long time. I knew Ben and the rest of the family almost as well as I did my own, except, of course, for Penelope. Never in all that time, even when you were left alone amid all that horror, did you seem less than sane and aware, when you were conscious at all.

'I cannot believe you had anything at all to do with freeing Ben's sister. It's to your credit that you feel the way you do. I can see that a decade of living with the thought might well convince you of things, which simply are not true. Things which are not logical!'

He chose his words carefully. 'I am asking you to do this because of our long friendship, as well as our business relationship. Look in another direction.

Tell yourself it is loneliness that has put this notion into your head. Explore the whole sequence of events again, minute by minute. Find the truth, if it takes you a year.' He smiled at her with all the warmth of his hope and his faith in her.

'Then open your door to the world again. You aren't old by any means, and you might find life still holding good things for your future.'

She smiled back, but the lines still marked her forehead. 'You are literally my only friend, except for Alistair, who is more like a son or a nephew by now. All right, Evan, I will think it all over again, I promise. Now bring out those balance sheets, before I lose all my nerve.'

★   ★   ★

The middle-aged man had come to the Clarrington house, opened the gate with his own key, and been admitted to the house. The watcher waited patiently, without moving, for he thought his involuntary motion of surprise had been detected by the visitor. He wondered who the man was and how he might gain access to that key, for the gate was the only feasible way to get into the grounds.

He knew, for he had checked everything out carefully, by twilight and dawnlight and moonlight. That damned electric alarm system to the fence was the problem. If he tried prying a couple of the iron spikes loose, the vibration alone, much less the movement of taking them out, would set the thing off. He'd met that kind of system before in his checkered career.

But there was his letter still to come. He felt that if it had been delivered already there would have been some sign from the tenant of the house. No, he had to allow time for the delivery, time for her to become fearful and nervous. Then he would get into the place.

He had decided the mailman was the easiest source of a key. He walked a long route, for the watcher had followed him, far behind or across the street so he wouldn't notice. It would be simple to waylay him someplace a long way from this quiet street at the edge of town. It would rouse no suspicions regarding this area.

His lair among the shrubbery of the vacant lot was becoming littered with candy wrappers and cookie boxes and discarded cigarette packs. He made a mental note to clean everything out before his last move. He wanted no clue to point to his being here . . . or to anyone being here.

The glance the man had turned in his direction had shaken him unduly. Had he seen a person in this distant clump of bushes? Or had he merely seen movement?

But the shrubbery was very thick, untrimmed for years, and the watcher had frozen instantly and remained still for a long time after the visitor disappeared into the house. If he had suspected anything, it was almost certain the stranger would have investigated.

Satisfied, the watcher lay back in his cushion of dead leaves, munching on peanuts. The climax was very near. He had waited so very long for this score.

It was almost time now.

★   ★   ★

Marise felt she knew her mailman, Mr. Neill, very well, though she had only communicated with him by way of notes for many years. He always rang when he had deposited the letters and turned the rotating drum that put the slot inside the entryway.

His solid shape, seen through the glass panels beside the door, was somehow comforting, a last connection with the world of life. If she needed stamps or had to sign for a letter from the Board, a note left in the box for him, or a ring on the bell for her, would take care of that without ever needing to open the heavy panel.

But she had expected no mail today. Her packet of new books wouldn't be due this soon, and nothing was expected from the Trustees. There was nobody who might write her casually, and Mr. Neill never rang the bell for junk mail.

Nevertheless, she heard the sharp ring clearly as she washed her few dishes in the kitchen. She wiped her hands on one

208

of Hildy's embroidered dish towels and hurried toward the entry and the mailbox.

A single small envelope lay in the compartment. Unfamiliar handwriting formed her name. Perhaps it was some newcomer to a local charity, demanding a contribution. She smiled, for it happened at times, and she always had the Board remind them that contributions came from the office, not the home.

Yet this was not the usual crisp, embossed envelope. It was, indeed, a bit grubby, as if it had been carried in a pocket for a while. There was no return address, and the postmark was from a nearby town, where she knew no one.

It was very odd. Intrigued, she ran her finger under the flap. Inside there were two sheets of cheap notepaper, the sort you bought at the supermarket in a plastic wrapper.

Marise took the letter into the parlor and turned on her reading lamp. Her eyes were not as strong as they had been, and she knew she needed glasses, but the handwriting was clearly formed and easy to read, though somewhat labored.

The letter had neither date nor return address. She read quickly:

Madam:

I have waited for years for this opportunity. Both you and I have been waiting, actually, though you haven't known it until now. I could have come before, might have rushed things, but the time had to be right for both of us.

Now things are right, for me if not for you. I know, you see, just what happened that night. You've never known for sure, and I've often laughed, thinking about you, trying to understand and failing. Too much had to have happened too fast. And you survived, which wasn't intended at all.

The two who did the work were the only ones intended to live through that night. They would have had everything: the money, the house, the business, all to themselves.

I owe you something. I was told about you by someone very close to me who knew you, what you did to that family and how you did it. You deserve to die, and I want to see it happen, feel it happen.

Look for me. Listen for me. It makes me happy to think of you shivering when the bushes scrape the house or the wind rattles the shutters. Jump at sounds. Be afraid. I am coming.

There was no signature. Marise stared down at the smudged paper. What could it mean? Had some crank dug up old files of news stories and decided to torture her? Or perhaps to rob her?

Who could resent her enough to condemn her as this letter had done? Only she had survived that night . . . unless that other, the mysterious presence who, through the years, had loosed Penelope from her prison, unlocking locks and sliding back bolts, had been in the house, too. Watching.

Was he watching now?

Marise shuddered. Dropping the letter onto the table, she went to the telephone and rang Evan Turner's office. Gertrude Fisk answered.

'I'd like to speak to Evan, please. This is Marise Clarrington.'

'I'm sorry, Mrs. Clarrington. Mr. Turner is out of town this week. Is there something *I* could do for you?' The voice was filled with curiosity.

Marise caught her lower lip between her teeth. Did she dare to risk telling Fisk about this letter? Evan had made it quite clear that she, more than the others who headed the corporation, was champing at the bit to find any excuse to remove the reins of Clarrington from her hands.

No, that wasn't prudent. It wouldn't seem sane to be so disturbed over an anonymous letter, even though there had never before been anything like it.

She made up her mind swiftly. 'Do make a note for him, will you? I'd like to talk with him as soon as possible, when he returns. I have had a communication I need to discuss with him. Be sure he gets your note, please, for I believe this may be important.'

Fisk said, 'Certainly, Mrs. Clarrington. You're sure there's nothing else I can do to help?'

'Thank you, but no.' Marise hung up the receiver, feeling the woman's curiosity still pulsing in her ear. She knew she should ask that the young lawyer be replaced with one she could trust, for an enemy connected with the Board of Trustees was not a thing she needed right now. Yet she couldn't bring herself to do that — not yet.

One thing Father Clarrington had made as an article of faith was fair dealing with the firm's employees. He had always bent over backward to avoid mistreating anyone employed by the company. No, Mrs. Fisk would stay, even at the risk of some danger to Marise's own authority. She had been too well conditioned to Clarrington ways to change now.

She paused. Should she seek further advice? She no longer knew anyone connected with the police or sheriff's department. Emanuel's old friend the sheriff was long dead, and even the shocked and sympathetic young police chief who had come on that last unforgettable night had now gone on to a better job someplace else. She felt unable to explain the entire affair, from beginning to end, to some newcomer who might think her completely unbalanced or incompetent.

She turned away from the telephone. No, if there was any real threat in that strange note, she must face it alone, as she had faced everything else these past years. As she had dealt with the horror of ghost-memories in this house.

Oh, how she needed Ben! More than any other time in these past years, she longed to lean on his strength and to consult his unfailing good sense.

★ ★ ★

Marise climbed the stairs wearily. Although the years had slid by so slowly, so quietly, leaving her hair ungrayed and her face unlined, she knew by the ache in her bones and her lessening vitality that she was aging. The steps she had run up with so little effort during the years when Ben was alive now seemed to have grown steeper and longer with the passing of time.

She could easily have moved into one

of the bedrooms on the second floor, which would have saved half a flight of climbing. Or she might have turned the small sewing room into a bedroom, and closed away the entire second and third floors of the house. But she had found herself unable to do that.

Now memories were her only companions. She had spent a significant portion of her life in these rooms. Closing away the past would narrow her present to almost nothing.

And Marise couldn't bear to give up any of the memories of Ben that lived in their tower apartment. The sitting room was so full of his presence, even after so long, she still looked up from her book or paperwork from time to time, thinking to see him in his recliner. He had rested there after his strenuous days, watching TV or dozing or reading the newspaper.

Their bedroom held even dearer recollections. They had known eleven years of marriage, a gift, she often thought, from Providence. Notwithstanding the things that came later, the years with Ben in these rooms had made up, just a bit, for what had happened.

Now she went up the last six steps that curved along the wall and stood on the wedge-shaped landing to open her own door. She had always loved the light there, for the tower, standing almost free of the rest of the house, caught the sun. Be it winter or summer, the windows held a blaze of skylight from dawn to dusk, for the big trees in the garden spread their broad limbs low and did not interfere.

The creamy walls, the rust and blue print of the curtains, softened the light without diminishing it. Her low antique bed, shaped like a boat whose prow-shaped foot curved gracefully to a small figurehead of a young girl, dominated the room. A matching chest and dressing table all but filled the available space, but there had been enough room there for a great deal of love.

Benjie had been begotten there, warming them with his too brief life. Their unique fires had burned there, for the years given to them.

She had learned to understand that it was fitting somehow. Illness had given

Ben to her, and it had been the same illness that took him away at last. There was a balance, a justice to the thought, painful though it might seem.

Dr. Pell sent Ben to a specialist at once, when he began to lose weight without any obvious cause. Hildy cooked like a madwoman, all Ben's favorite dishes, and Aunt Lina made up herb teas from the fragrant plants in her garden patch, and coaxed him to drink them.

Benjie had been old enough to understand something was amiss with his father. He'd taken to following Ben's every step, when he was at home, and whenever school was out he went to the forest with him as well. Marise's comfort, now, was to hope the two were together in whatever life might come after this one.

As for herself, she had simply dug in her heels for another battle to the finish for her husband's life. She had thought this time too, she might win that contest with death, for the first had looked even less promising. Then Ben had been underweight, hadn't eaten properly for years, and was terribly ill when he finally went to a doctor.

But after these intervening years he had been well-fed, his body was hardened by physical work, and he was surrounded with a loving family who struggled to help his body fight that nameless enemy. And it was still nameless, for even the specialists couldn't identify it.

Allergists had followed internists. Surgeons had explored. Technicians had drawn enough blood to satisfy Dracula without finding what it was that was draining the life from Ben Clarrington.

He had died, inch by slow inch, withering from a slender six-footer to a wasted figure that Marise had no trouble in lifting and turning. His flesh melted away over many long months, until only his black eyes still held a spark of his old self.

Long before she would admit defeat, he had known this was the last fight of his life. Even now, she could see him lying there, black hair and black eyes the only contrast to the pale sheets, so thin and colorless had he become.

A week before the end he called her to

his side. 'I want to talk to Benjie,' he said. 'He knows I won't make it, though he seems to be denying it to himself. It'll be easier if I tell him the truth, in plain words. It wouldn't be fair for me to die without letting him know what's coming soon. Tell him to come up as soon as he gets home from school.'

She had, of course, though the hardest thing she had ever done in her life was to turn her back on their room and leave Ben and his son to talk alone. Yet it was their right to be alone for this terribly private discussion. She had managed to give them that.

She had gone right down the stairs and taken refuge in Hildy's kitchen, crying on the cook's solid shoulder. Bless Hildy. She had been the only one who hadn't protested Marise's decision to nurse Ben to the end, right there in the room where they had been so happy. Marise had been determined he would die in his own bed, rather than in some sterile hospital room.

'Is best,' Hildy had said to Lina and Evan Turner. 'Hospital can do nothing. Doctor can do nothing. Is no pain. Why should he not be at home with us who love him? Marri is nurse and can do what he needs better than anyone else. Is best!'

That had quieted Aunt Lina's objections, and those of the Trustees, who already were running a large part of Clarrington Enterprises. But Lina never gave up hope. She seemed to feel that someone, somewhere, could keep her nephew alive. Yet, in the end, even she realized that for Ben, in his present condition, prolonged life would only be a cruelty.

Except for Penelope, everyone in the house visited Ben every day. Andy came faithfully, awash in whiskey fumes. He nodded and grunted and twitched his bushy eyebrows in the code Ben understood fully as well as Hildy did. Hildy came too, of course, several times each day, although the effort of hauling her bulk up the steps on those aching legs must have been torture.

Aunt Lina spent a lot of time there, with a book to read aloud or her sewing, while Marise was busy in the house or out at the farm. His aunt's presence had seemed to quiet Ben more than anyone's at the last.

Benjie visited morning and evening. After the conference with his father, the boy had cried to Marise, 'Why does he have to die? Why does everybody die? Uncle Hanni . . . I remember him, Mama. He wouldn't talk to me, and his eyes didn't see me. And Grampa died, and Grandmother and Miss Edenson. Everybody dies in this house. You're a nurse. You could stop it, if you wanted to!'

It had hurt desperately at the time, though she came to understand his childish anger. To his young mind she had seemed all powerful, as her own father had seemed to her at the same age. She had tried to explain, and he quieted at last, but still she sometimes caught a strange and thoughtful expression on his face. A judgmental expression, she thought.

Time would have taught him better, of course, but he hadn't had time. The memory of his fury and anguish still troubled her.

Marise thought it was Ben's illness and Benjie's pain that filled the house with such gloom and foreboding. Her eyes opened each morning to a new day, but there was no trace of her old joy. Reality pounced on her instantly as she rose from the cot beside the bed where Ben slept in drugged relaxation.

Grief, dread, frustration harried her through her days. Many of the nights were sleepless ones, despite the medication Dr. Pell had prescribed, and even when she slept nightmares hunted her through the hours of darkness.

Without the tranquilizers there would have been no sleep, she knew, even the broken kind from which she roused frequently to listen hard for Ben's labored breathing. When there was too long an interval between those breaths she came upright to check his pulse.

She too lost weight, which caught Aunt Lina's attention. It had been Lina who sent her off to Pell again for stronger medication, and those pills had helped. But it had been they, she thought, that caused those increasing lapses of memory that troubled her so deeply.

Pell had advised putting Ben in the

hospital, of course. 'Not that you aren't doing all that can be done, my dear, but because it is literally killing you. I can see that without any more examination. Since I saw you last you have dropped at least ten pounds and gained ten years.' He took her hand and shook it gently for emphasis.

'It would be so much easier for you. I know Lina and Hildy do all they can, but the burden falls directly on you, day and night. Do let me admit him.'

She remembered shaking her head, stubbornly determined not to give up until the last possible moment. 'Thank you, Doctor, but no. I understand your concern, and I appreciate it. Truly I do. But if I sent Ben away from home now, when he needs us most, I'd never be able to live with myself afterward.

'My husband is going to die in his own room and his own bed. With, God willing, his family gathered around him.'

But it hadn't quite worked out that way. She knew for two days that he couldn't last very much longer, and she kept Benjie home from school so he could be with his father as much as possible. Though Ben was too weak to talk much, he enjoyed watching the boy describe ball games or expeditions to the zoo or as he caricatured his teachers.

Benjie seemed to understand that his chatter pleased his father, and he seemed to generate it naturally. But one evening she found her son crying bitterly in his room, after a session with Ben. To her pained surprise, she knew he had been putting on an act to keep Ben occupied and amused.

He refused comfort, turning from her to bury his head in his pillow. 'Go away,' he sobbed. 'You can't help. You won't help him. Go away!' He hiccupped and wiped his tears onto the pillow case. She touched his wet cheek, but he drew away from her hand.

Ben died that night. Even full of tranquilizers, she heard the change in his breathing and knew he was in trouble in time to wake and try to help.

His struggles for breath cut through her heart, as she rose from her cot and went to his side. The night light showed his dark eyes, wide open, looking past her at something she knew she would not be able to see even if she turned. His hands rose toward her, and she clasped them against her chest.

'Tell Pen . . . ' he gasped. 'Tell Pen . . . '

'I'll tell her anything you want, Ben. What do you want me to say? I'll go as soon as I can. Ben! Ben!'

But he had already gone away from her, his hands going limp, his eyes flat and empty. The labored breaths rattled to a stop, and the struggles of his heart no longer twitched the cloth of his pajama top.

Marise laid his hands, now so uncharacteristically still, across his chest. She bent and kissed Ben's forehead and pulled the sheet over his face, after closing the staring eyes.

He had died in this room. Of all the deaths that had taken place in the house, his had been the only one she could swear was completely natural. Even Mother Clarrington's had left a question with her, after Edenson's talk of hearing voices in the night.

There was something . . . was it the house itself that seemed threatening? It had not been the people, for she had loved them all, excepting only Penelope, whom she had feared.

Had she feared Marise Dering? Had the strangeness emanated, in some way, from her own troubled spirit?

Marise shook her head and crumpled the ominous letter in her hand. Then she straightened it smooth and laid it on the nightstand beside her pale blue telephone. Evan would call, when he returned.

Until then she must take his advice. Painful though it was, she must relive that last terrible event in this house. She must examine every aspect of each incident, every reaction of the people involved, including her own reactions.

As for the threat in the letter, she must ignore that. Whatever happened now would have to happen, for there was nothing at all she could do about it.

8

POSTMAN FOUND DEAD

The body of Floyd Neill, 41, of 811 Postoak Grove Road was found at 11:00 A.M. on Friday, August 3, in a vacant lot in the 2000 block of Grapevine Street. Neill, a postal carrier for eighteen years, had begun his round normally. Deliveries were made over half his route, and his mailbag was almost half full when he was found.

Elmer Nichols, 18, of 830 Grapevine found the body while chasing his dog, which had run into the lot.

Police reached the scene almost immediately, as Nichols hailed a passing patrol car half a block from the scene of his grisly discovery. Police Chief Roger Tory has withheld the cause of

Neill's death, pending investigation by the coroner's office.

Neill's widow, Alice, told reporters she knows of no physical condition that might account for her husband's sudden death. Funeral services will be held at Offberg Funeral Chapel, time and date pending.

DEATH RULED MURDER
SUSPECT SOUGHT

County Coroner Warren Slote has found Floyd Neill, 41, postal carrier found dead on his route last Friday, to be the victim of strangling. Police have given no hint of a reason for the slaying. Neill habitually carried little cash when on his rounds, and his wallet was untouched. Several money orders were found among the mail left in his bag, ruling out the possibility of robbery as a motive.

Neill, an eighteen-year employee of the Postal Service, was well liked by fellow employees. Intimates insist he was happily married, regular in his habits, and had no known enemies. His widow, Alice Gerber Neill, is presently unavailable for comment.

The only clue police mention is a ripped inner pocket of the mailman's jacket. Fellow employees insist the jacket was intact before he left the Post Office on Friday. The rip seems fresh and indicates that some item may have been taken from the pocket.

A fairly tall, dark man was seen in the neighborhood earlier on the morning of August 3 by a resident of the street, who was walking his dog. So far, no other stranger has been reported.

Police Chief Roger Tory has neither confirmed nor denied that this stranger may be a suspect in the slaying.

NEILL MURDER STILL UNSOLVED
WIDOW GRANTS INTERVIEW

Alice Neill, widow of Floyd Neill, the postal employee found murdered last week on Grapevine Street, spoke to this reporter this morning. Mrs. Neill, who is not a suspect in the case, insists that her husband was a man of quiet and easygoing habits, well liked by neighbors as well as by those with whom he worked. She insists she can find no reason why anyone he knew should kill him.

Detailing his habits, she told this reporter that it was his invariable rule to stop to rest in the lot where his body was found. The stone bench under a tree at the rear of the grounds, which some may recall as the Olney property whose house burned three years ago, was his usual resting spot. At times in cold weather she would meet her husband there with a Thermos of hot coffee.

Mrs. Neill insisted that anyone who watched her husband for several days would surely know the time he would arrive, which was between nine and nine fifteen, six days a week. She maintains that he may have been killed for an item he carried in the torn inner pocket of his jacket. Only personal items were found by police, but Mrs. Neill claimed that he kept another there, a heavy key. She was uncertain as to its use. Police Chief Roger Tory refused comment when asked for reactions to Mrs. Neill's statement.

A funeral for Neill was held at Offberg Chapel on Tuesday, August 7, at eleven o'clock.

★   ★   ★

Marise seldom read the *Clarion* when it arrived. So little happened in Channing that there simply wasn't much local news, and national subjects were better covered by the Charlottesville papers Evan brought her from time to time.

She still subscribed, as the Clarringtons had for generations, and the paper arrived every afternoon.

The newsboy always flung it into the mail slot from the street, seldom missing his aim, though she had to turn the thing herself to get the publication out again. Sometimes it waited there until the next day's mail, but on Wednesday she usually took out the accumulation for the week to check for specials she might want Alistair to pick up for her.

When she unrolled the sheets the name Floyd Neill jumped out at her. She looked at the date, which was Tuesday's. The date of his death was the preceding Friday.

She read with concentration, a prickly unease spreading through her. Then she turned to page 3. NO FURTHER CLUES was the headline of a short paragraph recapitulating the story of Neill's murder.

Marise scrambled through the pile of rolled-back issues and arranged them in order of their dates. Then she began with the first account of Neill's death and moved forward chronologically. The story unfolded inevitably.

When she was done she leaned back in her chair. That inner pocket was the one in which he kept the key to her gate. Through the glass panels, she had often seen him fumble in his jacket and bring out the big key to unlock the gate. Despite the humid August heat, she felt a chill run up her back.

Marise reached for the telephone, dialed the number on the plastic overlay, and waited.

'Channing Police. Edgeware.'

It was a young voice. Too young? She had to risk it. 'Is the chief in? Chief . . . ' She looked again at the paper. 'Tory?'

'Jussa minute. Who's callin'?'

'Mrs. Clarrington. 317 Myrtle Street. About Mr. Neill, the postman.' Again she waited.

After a long buzz a deep voice said, 'Roger Tory here. May I help you?'

She took a deep breath before answering. 'I don't really know. I just read in the *Clarion* about the death of Floyd Neill, my postman. I am Mrs. Marise Clarrington. I live in the big stone house on Myrtle Street.'

'I know the family, yes, Ma'am,' he rumbled. 'What's the problem?'

'I am not really certain at this point that there is one. Did you happen to find among Mr. Neill's personal items a rather large brass key with the number 317 engraved on its shaft?' She felt a surge of almost-panic as she thought what it might mean if it had been missing.

'He had a key to my front gate. You may be familiar with the tall iron fence with the matching gate that surrounds my property. The key allowed him to get in to deliver my mail. I wondered about it. One doesn't like to think of a . . . a murderer who strangled a postman walking around with your key in his possession.'

'Hmmm.' She had a mental picture of a big, florid face, frowning perhaps, the eyes speculative. She could almost hear his wheels turning as he thought about what she had said.

'We didn't find a key, Mrs. Clarrington. We'll look among his things at the Post Office, and we'll keep in touch. All right?'

She could hear skepticism mixed with concern in his fruity voice. Clarrington Enterprises, the largest employer in the county, swung a lot of weight. Despite her oddities, Marise was the head of that concern. She could hear him biting down on the ideas of power and money.

But she also intuited his other thought. She felt him searching among his memories of stories about the old tragedy and the death of her sister-in-law Penelope.

'Thank you. I shall call again, if you

don't mind,' she said.

The phone clicked into place and she sat staring at the wall. Whatever happened in this house ten years ago, whatever part she might have played without knowing it, she now knew with total certainty that she had nothing whatsoever to do with Floyd Neill's death.

This might be cold comfort, but it was better than nothing.

⋆ ⋆ ⋆

He lay in his room, chuckling silently. The conversation he had just overheard as he passed quietly up the stairs to his cubbyhole had almost brought a snort of laughter from him.

Ellie, his landlady, was trying to pump information from Don Glass, the police dispatcher who lived in the third floor front. She was talking so fast, at first, that Glass had no chance to answer her, and the eavesdropper had paused on the landing to listen.

'I saw a police car across the street from her house this morning. What's going on, Don? I always did think she was too high and mighty to be real. Is she in trouble?'

'Now, Ellie, you know I can't give out that kind of information. Chief Tory just said to look over the house, see that the fence is sound and everything's okay. Old man Neill's murder has us all jumpy, and she called the station the other day and asked to talk to the chief. Probably wanted him to tell her everything was okay. God knows, you do the same thing to me, every time I come or go.'

Ellie snorted. 'I still think she's one to watch, for more reasons than one. You hear about people living alone and going nutty, every so often. Shooting into crowds or cutting folks' throats at night. Somebody who's lived alone for ten years has got to be squirrelly.'

Don didn't answer, but pretended to fumble with his room key. 'I hear tell she's a tiny little woman. Frail. Neill was a big fellow and would be mighty hard even for me to strangle. Nobody small could have got him.' But he never answered the woman's charge, and the watcher had run on up the steps on soft-shod feet, his shoulders shaking with laughter.

It was reasonable that people should suspect her, he thought. She seemed to be a pink monkey among all the brown ones, and they'd be sure to hate her and want to tear her to bits. She was different, and that meant dangerous. He rolled over and laughed into his pillow.

When he'd laughed himself out, he sat up to gaze out of his window. He could see, just barely, the tower of the Clarrington house, if he peered out sideways. The shape of that round tower sobered him.

A familiar fury washed through him, engulfing him in a flood of fire and blood.

★　★　★

Although she had not gone near Penelope's room in years, Marise remembered the chamber far too vividly for her own comfort. Only twice in her life had she visited the place, and the first time she had been so shaken she had not taken any clear picture of the rooms away with her.

Her second visit had been even more traumatic than the first, for she had gone to tell Penelope of her twin's death. She had approached the many-bolted door with her senses keyed to fever pitch and her nerves strung too tightly to bear. She remembered fumbling in her pocket for the key to the big lock and turning it, hearing the tumblers click. Andy, behind her, had cleared his throat gruffly and reached to undo the bolts.

She recalled noticing for the first time the smell of dust, linseed oil, turpentine, and the oily scent of paints. But another odor, faint and pervasive, also had reached her. She had noticed it every time she had encountered Penelope, though it was stronger here. She had unconsciously labeled it the smell of madness, though once she thought about it she knew it was ridiculous.

She had moved out of the corridor, which was dim even with the flower basket lamps on. Going into the room, whose skylight allowed the blaze of natural light needed for painting to pour through, almost blinded her.

Penelope had stood against the door leading into her bedroom, evidently drawn from her inner lair by Marise's knock. Tall and dark, strong and agile, she seemed unsure of herself and defensive. Her shoulders were huddled as if to protect her from some attack, as she watched Marise approach her. She ignored Andy completely.

Marise remembered the dryness of her throat, the tightness in her chest as she said, 'Pen . . . Penelope, I have come with very bad news. It's hard for me. It's going to be terribly hard for you too. Please sit down, won't you?'

The woman nodded and moved to sit on the small couch. Marise perched on a low chair, facing her. And though Marise was intent on her grief and the difficulty of conveying this new death to Penelope, the room swam into focus and she had to glance around. It almost took her breath.

'Penelope, how beautiful those paintings are! I never realized how wonderful your work is!' she had gasped.

For the walls were covered with

canvases, and its corners were stacked with more. Abstract designs of intricate color variations jostled dreamscapes that were infinitely detailed, real or misty, bright with the blaze of day or dim with the silver of moonlight. Whatever other tragedies it had achieved, the Clarrington heritage had produced at least one authentic genius.

But her words meant nothing to her sister-in-law. 'What do you want?' Penelope asked, her voice harsh and hostile.

Despite her determination to remain calm and in control, Marise felt her eyes fill with tears, but she blinked them back sternly. 'Penelope, Ben died early this morning. Before daylight. His old illness that he had when I met him . . . it came back.

'We took him everywhere, to any specialist we could find. Nobody could ever diagnose his problem, and this time was no different. Nobody could cure it. He's been getting weaker for a long while, and now he's dead.'

She gulped, wiped her eyes, and said, 'His last words were, 'Tell Pen . . . ' but he didn't last long enough to tell me what to tell you.' Now the tears flowed uncontrollably, though she managed to keep her voice even. 'He's to be buried tomorrow at ten o'clock. He'd want you to be there. Will you come?'

Penelope stared at her, through her. Those black eyes blazed with something Marise couldn't understand . . . was it excitement? Hatred? Triumph? She couldn't be certain.

But his twin must come to Ben's funeral, she knew, dangerous and unwise though it might seem. They had been born together and she deserved to see him buried.

Marise felt her sister-in-law controlling herself. It was like an electrical field in the room, making her own hair prickle on her scalp. The vibrations of those taut nerves veiled the room and even Andy squirmed. But Penelope only looked at her visitors, those eyes bright with unspoken things that neither could interpret.

But after a very long pause she said, 'I'll come. Tomorrow. At ten.' She rose and turned away from them, moving to an easel in the corner. She began squeezing colors from tubes onto a stained palette.

After that interview, Marise had never returned to Penelope's rooms. Andy had gone up and brought the madwoman down for the funeral the next morning, and she appreciated his sparing her the effort.

Now, after all those years, the paintings came back to haunt her. I should have had someone appraise them, she thought. I should send them to a gallery or an art dealer, even though she has been dead for a decade; such work has to command a market. It's such a waste, leaving them up there at the mercy of the damp.

A random thought floated through her mind. What was it Penelope intended to paint, that last morning? She had approached a blank canvas, but there had been purpose in her attitude, and her hands had been sure as she put color onto her board.

Marise thought of the note on her nightstand. It was a threat, she had no doubt. The postman who had brought it was now buried in the same cemetery holding the rest of her own family. She might as well end things tidily, if it came to that.

She would go up and look into Penelope's rooms at last, for better or worse. It couldn't hurt her worse than any of the other horrors she had already borne. And such a visit might explain something. You never could tell.

She turned toward the third floor for the first time in years. The corridor beyond the hospital suite was a disgrace, cobwebs festooning the cornices and dust dimming the carpet. It smelled musty, unaired. She should have hired someone to come in, at intervals, to take care of the worst of the dirt in the unused part of the house.

Marise sneezed, the sound sharp and startling in the stillness of the third floor. The blank doors of empty rooms seemed to echo the sound, and she shook herself.

Fancifulness had not carried her through all those years. Only hard self discipline and her own peasant stamina had done that.

She moved along the corridor and found the cross passage where she turned toward Penelope's rooms. The door stood open, as Andy must have left it on that last morning.

She didn't dare to hesitate outside, or she might turn and run away down the flights of stairs and out the front door. She pushed the door wider and stepped into the room where Penelope Clarrington had spent almost the entire span of her life.

Her easel still stood, back to the north light. The palette, its oils caked and dusty, lay on the little table beside it. Brushes stiff with old paint and dust stood in a jar from which the turpentine had long since evaporated. There was still a faint tang in the air recalling linseed oil and paint.

Marise crossed the room, her heels clicking sharply on the uncarpeted hardwood. She moved past the little sofa, the chair in which she had sat to tell Penelope her brother was dead. She went around the table and stared at the canvas on the easel.

A hand seemed to clench about her

heart, squeezing it painfully. She backed blindly toward the window seat and plopped down amid a puff of dust and mold.

Penelope's last work had been a portrait. The genius that had been her gift permeated it, gave it life even beneath the coat of dust veiling its intense colors.

At first Marise thought it was a likeness of Ben, remembered from their youth by his twin. The dancing black eyes stared from the canvas in their old familiar manner. But when she looked more closely, she realized the shape of this face was subtly different. The hair lay smooth instead of kicking up into rebellious curls.

This wasn't a portrait of Ben at all. It was a likeness of Benjie. And that was impossible.

Marise sat still on the window seat, her eyes fixed on the picture. Her mind was racing. As far as she knew, Pen had never laid eyes on Benjie until the morning of Ben's funeral, yet the woman had turned her back on her visitors and begun work on this canvas immediately after being told of her brother's death.

They had all known Penelope got out of her rooms at times, and it had been a constant worry to everyone. But when did she see Benjie? She had usually been out at night. Hadn't she?

Her son had never mentioned seeing his aunt, though it had been explained to him that she was very sick and had to stay upstairs. They had to tell the boy something, for he was too quick and curious to miss the fact that food was taken up three times a day.

How did she see him without his knowing it? Marise wondered. Or did he know he was being watched and keep it a secret?

Marise rose and lifted the portrait down off the easel. Carrying it carefully, she took it downstairs to her rooms, where she cleaned it with a soft cloth and soapy water. As she worked, she saw the tangled colors of the background clear and brighten and sort themselves, under her probing gaze, into another face. It was almost hidden in dreamy clouds of color, but it was Penelope's own, staring out of the canvas over Benjie's shoulder.

The expression was unlike any she had ever seen Penelope wear. Focused. Alive. Triumphant?

Marise dried the canvas with a towel, blotting it carefully before she leaned it against the wall and stood back. For her sanity's sake, she had to explore her memories of that last terrible day. Perhaps when Evan called her she might have something useful to tell him.

* * *

The morning of Ben's funeral had been cloudy, threatening rain at any moment. The services were held in the Clarrington parlor, and had been attended by a few close friends and one very distant and very ancient cousin, the last remaining Clarrington except for Aunt Lina, Penelope, and Benjie.

Evan Turner, young as he was, had been her right hand in attending to such matters. He had arranged, as Aunt Lina insisted, to have the body held at Offberg's until time to go to the cemetery. Despite the weather, the timing had gone off well, and the cars from the house had pulled up just behind the hearse. Marise thought it strange that such an irrelevant detail had stuck in her memory when she had been, she would have sworn, blind and deaf with grief.

There had been a canopy over the grave, the raw earth hidden by blankets of artificial grass and ranks of flowers. The small procession followed the pallbearers into its scanty shelter and stood while the coffin was set into place.

Although Evan indicated a bench at the front, Marise did not sit, nor did anyone else. It was as if they stood at attention for Ben while the minister who had christened him said a short prayer and intoned the Episcopal service for the dead. As he spoke, the rain began falling softly, then harder, and they turned at his final prayer and made for the cars.

Marise had been so weary and so sad that she clung to Benjie's hand, noticing only irrelevant things like the timing and the rain and the warmth of Benjie's small paw in her own. He squirmed from time to time as if to pull free, and she knew this alien ritual had not really served to help him bid farewell to his father. He was too young to grasp the full impact of what had happened to their lives.

Andy and Hildy had stood at the rear of the family group, together with a strange man whom she took to be someone hired to look after Penelope. She stood between the two servants, with the guard just behind her. When the group turned to leave the gravesite, those four led the way, picking their way over the damp grass and the graveled walks between the tombstones.

They reached the curving drive where the cars waited, and Penelope stepped forward calmly, as if to enter the limousine. Instead, she jerked her arm from Andy's unsteady hand and darted forward, stiff-arming the driver out of her way. She dashed around the vehicle as Hildy's shriek seemed to spur her to greater speed. Then she was gone across the drive and into the maze of plots and trees and headstones beyond it.

Marise stood frozen, and around her everyone else seemed frozen too. Nobody stirred to give chase for what seemed an endless moment. Then the young guard ran after her through the thickening mist, followed by the patrolman who had led the procession on his motorcycle.

That instant had cost them dearly, for it gave Penelope all the lead she needed. She bounded out of sight into the trees bordering the far side of the cemetery.

Aunt Lina, standing beside Marise, grasped her elbow painfully. The bruise lasted for weeks afterward, she recalled. 'Oh, Marri, if she gets away! She has no idea how to survive on her own. She can't know where she is or what to do to find her way home again, if she should want to. She's never been off the grounds alone since she was ten years old!' The woman's voice cracked.

'God, let them catch her! She is dangerous!' It was not an exclamation but a prayer, and Marise recognized it as such.

As long as they could see the bobbing heads of the pursuers, they stood in the rain, watching. At last Benjie tugged his hand loose and darted forward. That woke her from her bewilderment, and she caught him, just, by the tail of his jacket.

'No, son. That's your Aunt Penelope, you know. We told you about her. She is too ill to know what she's doing, and you can't help her. I'm not even sure they can catch her, and they're grown and have long legs.' She caught his reluctant hand again.

'We must get into the limousine right now and go home. We're all wet and we'll get sick too.' She managed, with Lina's help, to put the struggling, distracted child into the vehicle, and the quiet young man from Offberg's drove them home as calmly as if he saw madwomen escape and go haring away from funerals every day of the week. Marise had been oddly grateful for that.

The drive home had seemed much longer than the few miles warranted. Marise had sat, hands clasping Lina's and Benjie's all the way, with her mind racing. She had known, intuitively, that those men would never catch Penelope. Her flight had seemed, once Marise looked back on it, entirely too well timed and coolly carried out to be the sudden impulse of a demented mind.

She had to delay thinking about it, however, when they arrived at the house, for neighbors and friends had lunch on the table when they got there. Explanations had to be made, of course, and Marise could see the thought of that escaped madwoman running like a blaze through the thoughts of everyone there.

Although few knew of the Clarrington heritage and the trauma suffered by the neighbor's child had never been laid at Pen's door, the rumors about poor Clara still survived among the older generation of Clarrington acquaintances. It made everyone extremely nervous.

It was with considerable relief that she had seen the cousin, the neighbors, and the elderly group of friends take their departure. That left Marise, Lina, and Benjie to their grief.

Hildy went down to her own quarters almost immediately, and Marise knew she was worrying about Andy. He was too old to go running around in the wet, chasing after their charge. But he did come in, damp and defeated, in the mid-afternoon.

This time his wordless code was not sufficient. He had to talk aloud in words, and the effort seemed to exhaust him more than those exertions in the woods and the fields.

'She got away,' he said. 'Chased her clean into the woods, over the fields, and into the woods t'other side. Woods go clean to Pear Ridge. Never find her now. God knows what'll happen to her. Got to lock the gate.'

He'd hurried away before any more words could be pried out of him. His key was in his hand, ready to secure the lock. Marise gaped after him until Aunt Lina touched her hand and pulled her into the parlor to set her down in a deep chair.

'Don't you see?' the old woman had asked. 'Now she's tasted freedom. She was unpredictable before, when the entire world was contained by her room or at least parts of the house she could reach before someone caught her. Now, who knows?

'She might murder us in our sleep. That's a possibility, Marise. Remember the family in England and poor Clara. It's in the blood. I asked our lawyer to tell the police to keep a watch on the house tonight. I've never admitted it before, but I'm terrified of Penelope.

'She's hated me since that day she was locked away. She believes I persuaded her parents to do that, after she attacked me. Ben told her many times that it was his insistence which finally made them act, but she never has believed it.' Lina was pale, the jade green eyes almost faded.

'I'm old, Marise. I used to be strong enough to cope with anything, but now I'm too tired. Tired and full of grief. I simply don't care, any more. But I don't want to die in any way Penelope would arrange for me.'

Not only the outer gate was locked. The house, too, was locked tightly, the shutters latched, and even the iron fence was inspected for flaws. Aunt Lina's lawyer phoned to say the police would send a car past regularly, all through the night, in case the runaway tried to come home.

Marise tried to persuade her son to stay

with her in the tower suite. 'It's so lonely there without your Daddy,' she told him. But the black eyes avoided hers, and he shook his dark head.

'My father is dead now,' Benjie said, his tone flat. 'Everything is different. There's no family any more, except for you and me and Aunt Lina. And Hildy and Andy, of course. It's just no good any more. I'd rather be in my own room.' His voice had been cold, almost hostile.

Though watery sunlight peeped through the clouds before sunset, night came at last. If the day had been incredibly long, the night was interminable. Alone in the round bedroom for the first time in years, Marise tried for a while to sleep, but even one of her tranquilizers hadn't helped.

She rose at last and tried to read in her sitting room, but she couldn't concentrate. She felt like a clock whose spring had broken, letting everything fly apart in wild spirals. She simply couldn't be still.

At last she went to the kitchen and heated water for tea. She took the hot brew into the study, locking the door behind her compulsively, and sat in

Father Clarrington's deep chair. Something of his steadfast quality still lingered there, and it comforted her, just a bit.

But the night was full of menace that reached for her, though she knew on some level of her consciousness that the pill she had swallowed was working to distort her perceptions and tweak at her nerves. She had to be busy, or she would go mad.

The company books had not been brought up-to-date in two weeks, because she had been so busy with Ben. If anything could put her to sleep it was those columns of figures, she felt sure. She remembered struggling through them, jotting down totals, seeing the figures blur before her eyes. She must have drifted off fairly quickly, with her half-filled teacup at her elbow.

Something had awakened her. Even after so many years she could still feel the start with which she had jerked back to alertness. She sat up, her cheek sore from resting on her knuckles.

The tea was cold, and she knew she had slept for some time. She felt lightheaded and dizzy, and it was dark, for the bulb in the desk lamp had evidently gone out while she slept. The darkness was relieved only by a trace of moonlight filtering through the open draperies at the rear window.

She rose from her cramped position and stretched. Perhaps she could go to bed now and sleep. Marise reached for the brass lever that unlocked the door, fumbling awkwardly in the darkness.

But the door was not locked. It wasn't even quite touching the jamb.

9

Marise pulled her sweater more tightly around her shoulders. The August heat had not been able to warm her since she began her quest backward through the years to that hideous day and night. She felt as if she were in a crypt, damp with old horrors and fears.

She lifted the telephone from the table beside her and touched the dial. Then she set it back in its cradle. No, she would not give in to this panicky feeling.

Evan would call as soon as he arrived. She could depend on that, if upon nothing else in her strange life. To call again so soon would merely give Gertrude Fisk evidence to use if she tried to bring her competency into question. Besides, the call was only an excuse.

Her mind was playing tricks, trying to sidle away from pursuing the task she was requiring of it. She didn't, on some deep level, truly want to know what had happened that night. Perhaps her sub-conscious knew quite well that she had abetted Penelope in her terrible work. Perhaps her conscious mind wanted to avoid realizing her own guilt.

She stood and went into the entry hall. That night had begun, for her, in the study. She had to go there and repeat every move, every thought. She must see again everything her eyes had found as she staggered out of the dark room.

She opened the door and, once inside, she turned and closed her eyes to recapture the darkness in which she had stood. The door had, most certainly, been open when she woke. Even disoriented as she had been, there was no doubt of that, although she could recall turning the brass lever when she went in, hearing it click as the locking mechanism snicked into place.

Those were two incontrovertible facts. It had been locked. It was open when she woke. No matter what the tranquilizer had done to her perceptions, that much was certain. *Certain*.

Following that old pattern, she opened

the door again and went into the entry hall. There had been a draught there, she remembered clearly. It had chilled her bare ankles beneath the hem of her robe. She had thought at once of the door closing off the apartment below.

Andy frequently forgot to close it, and a draught pulled through the hall when that was done, because of the vent fans in the basement apartment. She remembered thinking about it, and that was another fact.

It had been entirely dark, though the fixtures along the stairwell should have been lit. She had left them on to cast their dim, warm light. Perhaps there had been a power failure.

She returned to the study, she remembered, and felt in the second drawer of the desk for Father Clarrington's huge flashlight. When she switched it on, its white beam cut through the darkness like a beacon. She followed it gratefully to the basement stair.

It had been terribly quiet down there, considering that Andy's snoring was famous for both volume and virtuosity.

When he slept, even catnaps in the daytime, the sonorous rasps often found their way to the entry hall, if the door was left open. But there was only silence.

The stair, too, stood in darkness, though its small light was never turned out. Marise set a foot on the top step and shifted her weight downward. She felt oddly disembodied. Worse than that, she had been filled with dread, for something had happened down there. Something she didn't want to see or even to find out about.

Reaching the middle of the stair, she shone the light downward toward the main door shutting off this part of the house. It stood open, and beyond it Hildy's door, too, was ajar, though the old couple usually sealed themselves into their quarters at night, whatever the weather.

Marise took another step downward. Something glistened on the floor just inside Hildy's doorway. It was shiny in the beam of the flash.

Sticky.

Red.

She had almost dropped the flashlight

as the smell reached her. It was not the familiar faint odor she had found so often in this house where so many had died. It was sharper, one she hadn't met in years, since her work in the operating room.

Blood.

Now she opened her eyes, almost feeling the shape of the flashlight in her hand, even after all those intervening years. She felt through her memories. What had she done at this point? Had she stood as she did now, paralyzed with terror?

She thought not. She should have stood frozen for only a few moments, though it might have been more. The medication had warped her time sense, she thought, and maybe it had distorted more than that.

She had to remember. She'd avoided thinking about this for too long, allowing it to trap her in this house, allowing her life to drift with time. She had taken refuge from herself even more than from the world. Now she had to know.

That letter had been the last straw. She

relaxed, allowing her mind to go back to her younger self, terrified, dizzy, filled with grief. Long or short, the time on the steps had ended at last, and she had rushed up to the entry, down the hall, into the kitchen. That light had come on without hesitation. So it was no power failure.

The kitchen had been ransacked. Drawers were left pulled out, spilling their contents onto the spotless floor. Cupboards stood open, their boxes and bags and cans disarranged. Someone had searched here frantically. For what? But even in her dizzy state she knew what had been done.

Drawn by instinct or memory, Marise had gone to the knife cupboard and looked inside. Two of the slots were empty. The carving knife that had reduced so many Christmas turkeys to bare bones was missing from its place. So was the cleaver. Even now she shuddered, remembering.

She had turned, feeling her robe swirling around her legs, and suddenly Aunt Lina's words came back to her with the emphasis of a shout. Shaken, she fled up the stair to the second floor, flicking switches as she passed, for all the flower fixtures had been turned off. They bloomed softly in that corridor as she reached the head of the stair.

She pounded on Aunt Lina's door, but it was not locked, though Lina had made a constant practice of locking herself in at night. That door, too, moved under her fists, and it swung open when she pulled at it. This made her stop short.

Always, they had locked their doors, Ben, Hanni, Father Clarrington, and Miss Edenson. With Penelope likely to escape from confinement, it was mad not to. Suddenly she didn't want to go into the room. She dreaded what might lie on the other side.

But she was a nurse, and she had bragged about her tough peasant heritage. She had the ability to cope with anything, come what might. Grasping the flash firmly, as much as a weapon as a light, she stepped into the room and switched on the light.

Her first thought was that Aunt Lina had repainted her room. But who would paint a bedroom red?

She reached to steady herself against the bureau and stopped just in time. It, too, was smeared with red. That could only be Aunt Lina lying there on the bed, and the floor, and the bedside table. But it was impossible to tell for sure now.

Marise's stomach had turned. No nurse or surgeon or even soldier had ever seen anything worse than that room. The worst thing of all was the giant painting on the wall facing the door. A great Cheshire cat grin was drawn there in shades of drying blood.

Her adrenalin had been flowing. Marise had felt her wits shake free of the clogging pill at last and throw aside the quaking of her own flesh. For she thought of her son. Benjie had been alone on this floor with Penelope, who must have achieved at last her long planned revenge against her aunt.

What had the woman done to her son? She turned, her robe flapping against the wet smears on bureau and doorjamb. Her heart tight in her chest, Marise had run for Benjie's room.

Caught in the grip of those old memories, Marise fled along the corridor to the room that had been her son's. They had not used the old nursery on the third floor, but had decorated one near the head of the stair with the gnomes, elves, and nursery story figures Marise loved when she was a child.

When Benjie was eight, he demanded that his walls be painted off-white. He favored a spartan style, with a camp bed, desk, folding chair. 'Like a safari,' he pleaded, after seeing a movie that caught his fancy. That was what they had done, and he had seemed quite pleased to let it remain that way.

She remembered running to this door and slowing to a stop. What would she find inside? Could she bear it if her son had suffered the same fate Aunt Lina had?

Then she had caught herself. Benjie might be in there right now, she thought, cowering in the dark, terrified of what he must have heard from the adjoining room where his great-aunt had died so horribly. She touched the knob and found this door was locked.

Her heart thudding with relief, she sped down to her own rooms and got the key from her desk, which also held spare keys to all the rooms in the house. As she turned it in the lock of Benjie's room she was crooning comfortingly, 'It's all right, darling. Mama's here, and it's all right. We'll pack right up and go back to New England.'

There was no sound from inside and she redoubled her assurances as the door opened. 'I'll get a job and we'll live in an apartment and have a wonderful life. Don't be afraid, son, no matter what you've heard. I'm here now.'

The light was on. Benjie wasn't in his room, though the bedclothes lay in a tangle, and his sneakers, which he insisted on using as house slippers, were not under the bed.

There was blood on the door knob, the pillowcase, and it had dribbled down the khaki colored counterpane.

Marise's knees went out from under

her and she sat abruptly on the floor. She could taste vomit, but when her stomach heaved nothing came up.

She gagged again. Then she drew a deep breath and called, 'Benjie! Benjie!' She knew with bitter certainty there would be no answer.

Nevertheless, she hauled herself upright and pulled open the closet door. Nothing there. She stooped and peered under the bed. No trace of her son was to be found in his room.

She asked aloud, 'What would . . . what could Penelope have done with him? I have to think like a crazy person. Where would I hide a little boy, living or dead? This house is too big — there must be a hundred places Penelope knew as a child but I could never discover. I've never even walked through all of it.'

She strained to think, to work her way into that demented mind. 'The attics? I never went there. Nor to the rest of the basements, beyond Hildy's apartment. There must be cubbies and crannies and closets I don't even suspect are there.

'Too many! Too many!' Tears had

streamed down her face, but she paid no attention.

Shuddering, her teeth chattering, she had torn herself from that empty room and run down the stair to her own landing.

She had to call for help. God grant that Penelope hadn't torn out the phone wires!

* * *

Marise could still feel the sick despair that had gripped her as she searched for her son. It had never, she realized, entirely left her. She'd carried its dregs in her soul through the intervening decade. Now it was part of her blood and bones, and she had not been consciously aware of it.

On that terrible night she had gone to earth like an animal pursued by predators. Her own place, her own rooms held the last remnants of sanity and safety in a world gone completely mad.

She tore her door open without pausing, for she had left it unlocked after finding Benjie's key ... the moment seemed years ago, now, instead of minutes. That hasty trip was a blur in her mind, for all her thought had been concentrated on the boy.

She recalled setting the automatic lock and pressing the light switch, before turning toward the phone table. Penelope stood there, smiling calmly, waiting for her in the center of her own sitting room. The missing carving knife was in her hand.

The dark pantsuit the woman had worn to her twin's funeral was now gaily patterned with scarlet and rust. Her fingers were dark with blood as well, and the underside of her jaw was spattered with it. The smile faded, leaving her expression quizzical ... the look of a cat regarding a mouse that had escaped, only to be caught again.

Penelope was big, stocky and powerful, and she knew her own strength. Her stance was easy but alert, as if she discounted anything Marise might do to resist her.

Marise understood; she was expected

to try to run, and any attempt at flight would be thwarted instantly. Suddenly her world shrank to the dimensions of this single room.

Time slowed. Grief and fright and anger chilled out of her consciousness as her mind frosted to a single point of survival. There was one chance for life, and she had to live until she found Benjie. She asked only that much of fate. Let her find her son, alive or dead, and she would die without a whimper.

Marise moved forward toward the watching, waiting woman. Penelope didn't expect her to do that, and her eyes narrowed. This reaction was not one she was used to, it was obvious. She backed a step, and her air of confidence diminished just a little. As Marise drew nearer she backed another step; perhaps she remembered the smaller woman knocking her unconscious, on their first encounter so long before.

Certainly Marise was remembering. She held to the thought with desperate tenacity. She had done it once, and she had to do her best to repeat her feat. That attack had been unexpected, however, and now Penelope was wary, recalling what she might do.

Only her training, Marise realized, could bring her out of this room alive. That and the cold sharpness her mind had become, razor-honed with desperate need. She had to lull Ben's twin, get her off balance, so she moved forward again, almost within reach of the madwoman.

Penelope stood almost against the curving wall of the sitting room now, and had begun glancing rapidly from side to side, as if she expected someone to attack her from behind and come to Marise's aid. Yet she had to know the two of them were the only living people in the house unless Benjie — but Marise pushed the thought aside.

Penelope stepped forward, her big hot body almost touching Marise. She had not flinched, Marise recalled with pride. Instead, she reached forward, almost casually, and whipped the carving knife out of Pen's hand. Without interrupting the motion, she flung it away behind her and heard it clatter against some piece of furniture.

'What did you do with the cleaver?' she asked, her voice glacially calm.

Penelope hadn't expected that or any question from her, it was obvious. She had become so used to being the silent, unseen terror, instantly imprisoned again when she was caught, that she didn't know how to deal with words. Almost solely in her own rooms had anyone spoken to her.

'I . . . left it . . . somewhere,' she faltered. Now the black eyes were wary, unsure of what she might expect. There was a flicker of something wild behind them.

Marise caught the signal immediately and stepped sideways, knocking against the phone table. Pen's rush carried her past, but Marise had no chance to strike her.

'You killed your father,' Marise said in a conversational tone. 'Didn't you?'

The woman turned, looking crafty now. 'I'm no fool,' she said. 'I knew too much of that medicine would kill him. I hoped they'd think you murdered him and would send you off to prison, but they didn't. Too bad.'

'And Miss Edenson?'

'How could I? I was locked up then and couldn't manage to get out. Still, I did . . . arrange it. Yes, I did arrange it, just like I did Mother. I made the plans and somebody else did the work for me. Wouldn't you like to know who?' The black eyes were mocking, and Marise felt a sudden rush of fury.

But Penelope moved before she could use any of the tactics she had been considering. She dashed toward the knife, out in the room, swooped upon it and turned again to face Marise.

'Now we'll see,' she panted. 'You came here into my house, married to my brother. You tricked them all into loving you too, though they never loved me. They locked me up, all alone, except for Andy. And he was only there part of the time.

'When Hildy told me about you I meant to kill you, right off, but I didn't have the chance. I only had time to fix your bridal chamber for you.' She smirked.

'Then you were gone so much, or

locked up in here with Ben . . . my Ben! I got out a few times and talked to you. You heard me too, didn't you? I hoped I could frighten you away, if I couldn't kill you, but you were too stupid to run. Now look what you've made me do!'

Though she heard the words, Marise was watching her eyes. When those moved off her face, she knew what she had to do, but she smiled carefully and said, 'You know better than that. Nobody made you do anything.' She took a deep breath.

'I don't believe in that famous Clarrington madness. I think what you suffered from was the old Clarrington greed, that grasping for things and money and power, but you carried it to an awful extreme. I wonder if the same wasn't Clara's problem, and the musician uncle's too. The old grabby tendencies that made cousins marry cousins for so long to get land, despite the odds, and that caused the problem.

'One in every generation got the benefit of that, it seems. The rest gave them the benefit of too many doubts, I feel certain.'

The black eyes shifted, just a fraction.

Marise reached behind her, tore the phone loose from the wall with a single pull, and met the woman's rush with all her strength behind the weight of the instrument.

Penelope stood for a moment, her ruined face filled with shock and surprise. The phone dropped from Marise's hand and she staggered back to lean against the wall. Now she had done her best, and it hadn't been enough.

Her sister-in-law took a step forward, but her foot crumpled beneath her. She fell onto her bloody face at Marise's feet.

Marise remembered . . . it had taken her some time to gather the strength to move. And in that interval she heard something on the stair. Had it been a footstep?

In this present, she still strained to remember the sound. She had been exhausted, drained, so battered emotionally and physically that she had hardly known what she was doing. Had she actually heard anything at all, or had her imagination, strained past belief, laid the groundwork for the trap in which she found herself?

In the time when she thought she was asleep in the study, had she herself opened the iron gate and the heavy front door for Penelope? Had some latent madness in her been drawn by that tragic woman to do such a thing? Was she driven to insanity by the losses she had sustained?

She sighed with effort, trying to remember. Was she guilty, along with Penelope, of the deaths of Hildy and Andy, Lina and Benjie, as well as of the death she did recall? She closed her eyes, straining toward that frozen moment in the tower room.

There had been something on the stair, and she had still thought so as she went down to the parlor to telephone for Evan Turner. Had it been a mouse?

Perhaps.

She barely remembered that phone call to Evan, who had become such a good friend while working with Ben in the woods. She knew he had suffered a bad night himself, after carrying Ben to his grave the afternoon before, but he had been the one she thought of and the one whose number she could remember without looking it up.

His voice had been fogged with sleep when he answered the phone. That was one landmark in the fog of the night. He must have had trouble going to sleep too.

She recalled her words quite clearly. 'Mr. Turner, can you come? We have a . . . problem here.' The understatement, when she thought of it, had left her half amused and half shaken for all the years since.

Later he told her he had come in a rush, to find the front gate standing open and the front door unlocked. Only the open parlor door had revealed that she was there, mercifully unconscious at last, beside the dropped phone.

Ten minutes later the patrol car had passed, having been delayed by a traffic accident on the other side of town. It had been the officer in it who found Hildy and Andy, or what was left of them.

He and Evan had searched the rest of the house as well. They'd found Aunt Lina, Benjie's empty room — and the remains of Penelope in the tower sitting room. 'It was like a nightmare,' Evan told her later.

'She still had the knife in her hand, glued fast with blood. She lay there with her skull smashed in and the broken phone beside her. God only knows how you managed to stop her with such an unlikely weapon.'

Of course there had been a lot of publicity, for the Clarrington name carried a lot of news value. The Clarrington flaw had been thoroughly aired, not only by the media, but by the gossips all over the state who had known any of the family.

Even Clara was dragged from her obscure niche in history and examined closely. Nothing could be proved at this point in the game, but speculations had struck very close to the truth. Marise realized that, weeks later, when she was able to read newspapers.

Luckily, nobody ever thought to investigate the British branch of the family and its terrible end. She was glad to let them lie, untroubled, in their graves. Their fates would have added a note of the macabre to the nasty situation.

Marise had been ill for a long time. Strain, her bad reaction to the tranquilizers, and shock had taken their toll, and that last night had been the final straw. Dr. Pell had sedated her and she was in the hospital, unconscious, while the investigation went on. She did not know when the bodies were buried, quickly and quietly, and the house returned to some sort of order.

The family had come to so sudden an end that there was no provision made for carrying on the full activities of Clarrington Enterprises. But the limited board of that time had been in place, and Evan had taken charge, with her short-term power of attorney, and proved himself to be so knowledgeable and competent she had decided, later, to put him in permanent control.

For she was, quite literally, the only heir. That distant cousin had died of a heart attack the night after Ben's funeral, leaving her Ben's heritage. Aunt Lina's interest had been left to Benjie, and it had also come to her as his surviving parent.

She organized the Board in the most effective way she could. And as almost the sole stockholder, she overrode all objections. Then she moved back into the house that had held all her happiness and all her nightmares, and closed its doors behind her.

She sighed. What had she dredged up from the past in this traumatic reliving of it? She could find only the things she had known before . . . or was there more? She had a feeling there might be, if she could find it.

One thing was certain. Someone had let Penelope into the house that night. If it had not been she, then who had it been? There simply was nobody else.

A sudden thought occurred to her as she rose wearily to face another night in the bedroom she had shared with Ben. She searched her memory, but she could find no answer.

I'll ask Evan when he calls, she thought, turning out the light and closing the door of the study.

10

Evan dialed Marise's number with some unease. He'd been feeling strange about her since their last talk before he went on his business trip. Mrs. Fisk's delayed message woke that uneasiness even more as he waited for an answer as the phone at the other end buzzed and buzzed.

'Clarrington House,' came the answer at last. Ah. 'Marise? Evan Turner. Mrs. Fisk said you called and asked for me to call back. She said you sounded disturbed, which seemed to please her a lot. But I hope it wasn't urgent. She didn't give me your message at once.'

When she spoke, her voice seemed odd. 'Evan, I've had a letter. A very strange letter. I'd like for you to stop by when you have the time and read the thing. It . . . upset me. I realize it may be from some crank, but it's been so many years since our tragedy that it seems unlikely. Do you mind?'

As if he ever minded! 'Of course not. I have news from our Washington lobbyist too. You were right, we hadn't approached the committee from the right angle. Your plan worked beautifully, and I think you'll be pleased.'

'Good.' Her tone dismissed that triumph, somewhat to his surprise. She'd been so intent on getting the results they needed. 'Evan . . . ' She sounded hesitant.

'Is there something else, Marise?'

Now her voice was thick, as if she were forcing her words past some inner reluctance. 'It never occurred to me to ask, and I know it sounds completely insane, but I never knew where you found Benjie's body. I couldn't make myself go to the cemetery, after, to see the markers.'

Even now, he knew that speaking about Benjie was almost more than she could endure.

'I wasn't able to think about my son at all. I shut what had happened out of my mind, and I knew it at the time. I just couldn't let it get close to me, if you see what I mean. That night I couldn't look for him myself, and it just now occurred to me — he was the only one I didn't find, or at least know for certain where he was.' She swallowed hard.

'I think I can handle it now. Will you tell me?'

Evan turned his head to stare from the office window at a rank of high clouds. He gripped the phone so tightly his knuckles whitened and his fingers almost numbed. Yet he managed to keep his voice quite calm.

'Look here, my dear, this isn't something to discuss over the phone. As I'm coming out anyway, why don't we talk about it after I get there. Can you wait?'

Her laugh might as well have been a groan. 'I've waited for ten years to ask the question. I should be able to wait for a few hours to get the answer. Certainly. We'll talk about it when you get here. Come by around five-thirty, after you leave the office, if that's convenient. I'll have . . . tea and cookies.' Her voice was trying for lightness, but she wasn't able to achieve it.

'I'll come earlier. By five, if that's all right with you,' he said. 'Okay?'

'Fine.' The receiver clicked in his ear, and he replaced the phone, feeling thoughtful. He felt himself frowning and deliberately smoothed the line from between his eyebrows.

He pulled his leather bound directory toward him and looked up a number. Then he dialed again.

'Forrest? This is Evan Turner. Do you recall our special inquiry some years ago? Yes, I agree. And nothing ever turned up? I see. No, not really, I just thought something might have surfaced at last. Thank you, Forrest. Yes, you too. Goodbye.'

But once the door closed behind him, Evan didn't give the inquiry another thought. All the time he drove toward Myrtle Street he was thinking furiously about what he must tell Marise Clarrington.

She might be angry, and he wouldn't blame her. She might slip off the tightrope she had walked for so long and become really unbalanced. Any one of a dozen things might happen. He hated to pull up to the curb and park in front of that massive gate.

It opened to his key, and he locked it carefully behind him. Too much had happened because this gate had somehow been opened at the wrong time. He was almost as compulsive as Marise about securing it.

He could hear the doorbell buzz in the entry, and Marise's familiar step sounded on the other side of the door that still snarled with jungle animals. When it opened he reached to take her hand.

'Marise. You look a bit worried. Are you all right?'

She looked up and nodded slightly. 'I took your advice, Evan. I relived every-thing that happened. It's . . . something of a strain, as you might imagine.'

But he thought she looked too pale and drawn for anything that had happened ten years ago, however terrible it might have been, to warrant. He followed her into the parlor and set his briefcase aside.

'Let's skip the tea this time, all right?' he said. 'You want two things from me. Which do you want to do first?'

She braced herself against the back of

her low chair. 'I want to know about Benjie. Where you found him. What . . . happened to him. Once I realized I never asked and you never said, it began haunting me. I can bear it, Evan. I saw Lina as Penelope left her, and anyone who could stay sane, more or less, after that can stand anything. Tell me. Everything, down to the last detail. Nothing you can say to me can possibly be worse than the things I have been imagining for the past night.'

Evan looked down at his hands, which had clasped involuntarily in his lap. He relaxed them with an effort of will. He knew she was watching him closely, and he tried to seem at ease, though he felt certain he was almost as tortured as she.

'If it is going to bother you to tell me,' she said, 'think about it while I get the tea. That will give you something to do with your hands, and it will warm you up inside.'

He couldn't argue with that. When she returned with the hot cup, he sipped gratefully. It was August and very hot, but he felt as if it might be winter, so chilled was he with the story he must tell.

'You asked for everything,' he began, 'and I'm going to give you everything, and when I'm done you may ask for my resignation, which you will be welcome to. But don't . . . don't interrupt me until I'm done, all right?'

She nodded. Her face was still, but her hands crumbled a cookie in her saucer.

'After I got you off to the hospital, that night, we began to search the house. Officer Burt was the one who looked down . . . down there. Hildy and Andy were both dead, carved terribly, but it was nothing like what she did upstairs to Lina. The young man was staggered, for he hadn't seen the other yet. He ran back up the stairs, yelling for the sergeant and me.' Evan cleared his thought and loosed his hand from the arm of his chair.

'We didn't notice until he was in the entry that he had blood on his boots. He tracked it onto the carpet.' Evan felt himself pulled back into the memory of that night. The tidy room went out of focus as he saw into the past.

'It warned us, of course, what was to

come. Once we found the gate open we feared the worst, but that didn't help much. He told us what was downstairs, and we looked up the stairs toward the second floor. He went pale, and I know the sergeant and I must have looked pretty sick as well.

'You had left all the doors open behind you. That helped us avoid wasting time looking in empty rooms. Benjie's door, nearest the stair, was the first we entered, and that wasn't so bad, except for the blood. But it was only blood, as I know you found for yourself.

'When we went into Lina's it was different. Burt vomited on the floor, and I would've, too, if I hadn't been so focused on finding what had become of Ben's son. We looked around on that floor, but all the other doors were unlocked. We knew there had been only five of you in the house, not counting Penelope. Four of you were . . . accounted for.

'We went down to the tower landing. The light was on, the door standing open. We could see Penelope's foot from where we stood before entering. The room was almost tidy, except for the ripped-out telephone. We could read what had happened without any trouble, for it was perfectly clear.

'You came there to call for help and found Penelope waiting. The blood on her hand had glued the knife to her skin, and we didn't try to force it out. We just looked, saw what you had done to save yourself, and went down to meet the police chief and the coroner. That was before Tory, of course. I can't recall that one's name without looking it up.'

He accepted a glass of water from the carafe on the table beside Marise and felt the cool liquid ease his dry throat. 'The chief asked me immediately if you could have had anything to do with the murders. I didn't have to say a word, for Burt made as fine and succinct a report as I ever heard. He'd noted exactly how much blood was on your robe and gown, and where it was located. He saw that your hands were clean. Not washed clean but not bloody. He cleared you of any part in the killings, and I didn't have to say one word.' He sipped water again, feeling his old gratitude well up in him. It had been a remarkable job for a youngster to do.

'You had a lot to thank him for, but he went on to a much better job out of state, before you were out of the hospital. Once the technicalities were out of the way, and with the murderer dead there was no need for a trial, he was free to take the offer that came almost at once.'

Marise opened her mouth, but he shook his head. 'I'm getting to it. Takes me a while, I know, but I am almost as hung up on that night as you are. I have to work my way into it, so to speak.' He sighed and set the glass down. 'We got a lot of help, and we went to work on the house and grounds. There was so much of it, and so many places where he might have been, but we looked for Benjie through every closet, floor by floor, cupboard by cupboard. And we found nothing.

'Then we did the grounds, and in the dark that was an incredible job. We took the rockery apart, stone by stone. I had someone put it back together before you came home. We dug in all the loose ground we could find. We even . . . looked up in the trees. And we found nothing.

'We knew one of two things must have happened. Either Penelope killed him and hid him so well there was no way for anyone who didn't know the house intimately to find him, or he saw what happened. His great-aunt's door was next to his, and he might well have heard something to bring him out to see. If that had occurred, he might well have run for his life, driven by a terror that could have caused amnesia.'

Now Marise spoke at last, sitting forward with color in her cheeks for the first time. 'You mean . . . he might still be alive?' Her voice trembled with unbelieving hope.

'It is possible. Just possible, no more.'

'But why didn't you tell me? I'd have searched the world over, done anything at all, whatever it cost. Why else should I have all this useless money?'

He leaned forward in turn. 'What do you think we have been doing? For ten years we've had investigators running down even the most trivial clue. You were in such a state when you got out of the hospital . . . well you can't remember, and I don't want to remind you of anything you're better off forgetting. We figured, and Dr. Pell agreed, that if you thought your son was dead — if you thought everything was ended for good, it would help you get your feet back under you.

'You're tough, Marise, and you did get them back. You got everything under control, took charge of the businesses, set the goals and met the challenges. I still think we did the right thing.' His gaze dared her to protest.

'Detectives have been working on this since the day after the tragedy. More than one agency on more than one continent has given it their best. The boy might have been frightened literally out of his wits. Who knows where he might have run to or who might have picked him up or taken him in?

'His description has gone all over the world. We turned every nearby town, from Deep Creek to Tolliver, upside down, and nobody had seen a child of his description. We couldn't find a single lead. There was nothing you could have done differently, if you had been managing the search yourself. And there it is.

'Either he is still right here, his bones hidden someplace only Penelope knew, or he's out there somewhere. If that is true, he probably doesn't remember who he is — or where he came from.'

He stared down at his hands. His knuckles were white again. When he looked up she was regarding him with a strange expression.

'Well?'

She shook her head. 'I suspect I would have done the same thing, in your place. I can't blame you. Probably I am just now able to take this in my stride anyway. Don't feel guilty, Evan. I understand.'

He sighed and reached again for the glass of water. She was still an amazing woman.

'Now what was that other problem you wanted to see me about? Some letter you got in the mail?'

She shook her head. 'Oh, that. It's not important, anymore. I threw it away after

I called you. I was ashamed of getting into a flap over nothing, I suppose.'

There was something in her voice, a shadow behind her eyes that troubled him, but Evan knew better than to try pushing his way past her guard. She had never allowed that.

But it bothered him all the way home.

★　★　★

The key worked in the iron gate. The watcher had tried it, waiting until after midnight to venture out of his nest of hedge bushes. The street was empty at that hour, and in this neighborhood of elderly people there were seldom any late cars to disturb such activities. He had memorized the schedules of the few night workers as well.

He'd slipped along the fence to the gate and the lock had turned noiselessly. Somebody kept it oiled, he knew at once. But it was not time yet. He had to do this with finesse and wait for the perfect moment to go to work.

Now he lay on his bed in the rooming

house, the key hidden under his pillow. As usual so early in the evening, the house was a bit restless. He could hear Ellie complaining to her husband in the room just beneath his. People came and went on the stair, their footsteps and voices irritating him almost beyond endurance.

Once in a while he would stick his head out of his door and greet one of the other roomers with false cheer, for it was important they remember that he was in his room this evening. He had to drive that fact home to more than one.

Glass, the police dispatcher, opened and closed his door, which was down the hall. He worked a split shift this weekend and he was on his way to work. When he reached the corridor outside the Watcher's room, the man opened his door and called, 'Don! Will you do me a favor?'

The dispatcher turned, smiling. 'Sure, Rick. What do you need?'

'Pick me up some cold tablets, will you? Doesn't matter what brand. I'm coming down with a cold, and there's nothing like late summer crud to lay you low. Just so it eases my sore throat and clears up my head, anything will do.' He fumbled in his pocket and pulled out a bill.

'Here's five. Is that enough?' He managed a hollow cough.

'No problem,' Glass said. 'I'll put the packet on the hall table, if you're asleep when I come in. I wouldn't want to wake you up, if you've finally drifted off.'

'That's fine. I usually hear your steps coming up the stair or your door closing. If I'm awake I'll go out and pick them up. Thanks, Don. I really don't feel like going out myself.'

Closing the door, he turned back to his narrow bed and felt the waiting key burning through the thickness of the pillow. It was almost time. Almost time . . . almost time.

★   ★   ★

Marise had read the letter until it was crumpled and stained with perspiration. She was certain she had been right to keep it from Evan Turner, now that she had all the threads in her hands at last.

Every instinct warned her something unbearable was coming. It was better to protect poor Evan from more pain.

The part of the house that she used was as neat, as dust free, as tidy as her hurried hands could make it. The kitchen was scrubbed spotless. The parlor shone, its cut glass and porcelain newly washed and the upholstery vacuumed.

Whatever was going to happen, the house would present a respectable front to anyone coming into it.

She went up to the tower apartment and bathed slowly and luxuriously, after the hard work was done. She changed into a neat jumpsuit and, sitting before the gold-mounted mirror Ben had given her, she brushed her fine, light hair a hundred carefully counted strokes. Then she stood and looked critically at her reflection.

She nodded. 'I've done the best I can,' she told the fragile shape in the glass. 'I understand, and God knows nobody on earth knows better than I, how messy death can be. But what can be done, I've tried to do. Now I can only wait.'

She turned her gaze toward the painting of Benjie, which hung on the wall beside the door. It stared out at her, the black eyes unreadable, filled with a sort of excitement she had not yet been able to understand. Behind his image the shadow image of Penelope's face seemed to grimace.

When had Penelope seen him like that? Or had the woman's fertile imagination conjured up from her own troubled spirit this vision she'd painted.

A shiver shook her, warm though the evening was. Penelope's face loomed behind the boy's head. Her look of triumph — what had she seen or dreamed to make her paint herself so?

Marise turned and left the room, descending to the study. There was still work to do, and she suspected her time was limited. She closed the door behind her and sat in the big chair behind the desk where Father Clarrington had spent so many busy hours. His father and grandfather before him had worked to build the empire that now rested in her weary hands. But it was about to change;

her instinct told her so.

She drew from a drawer a pad of lined yellow paper. At the top she wrote in firm letters,

LAST WILL AND TESTAMENT OF *MARISE DERING CLARRINGTON*

August 28, 1997

She wrote for a long time. She knew the legal system could undo even the most careful of wills, given sufficient reason and pressure; forty-seven million dollars, plus hundreds of thousands of acres of timber and farms and rental housing would be, she was sure, more than enough to snare lawyers into trying to make a change.

Again she bent over the pad, her pen busy. This was not to be a will, but it would put the management of Clarrington Enterprises fully into the control of Evan Turner, reducing the Board of Trustees to a purely advisory body with each member responsible only for keeping up with the specific area of the business he had been chosen to oversee.

Evan had been patience itself, all these years, asking nothing in return. Yet if power could reward him, she could provide that. She doubted, in her heart, that this document would substitute for that for which he had never asked. However, it was the best she could do.

When she was through she read both documents through three times, changing a word or a punctuation mark, making the necessary corrections. Then she signed and sealed them into a large manila envelope marked —

FOR EVAN TURNER IN THE
EVENT OF MY DEATH

She took it to the big, old-fashioned safe hidden behind a coy painting of a nymph who was trailing strategically placed draperies. The combination was automatic, by now, as she twirled the dials, turned the knob, and looked into the oily smelling depths of the monster.

A grown man could have hidden inside it. The right side consisted of dozens of narrow shelves, and across the bottom were two large drawers, with individual locks. On the left was ample space for bags of gold or bundles of currency or whatever valuables might need safe-keeping. With so much space, the small bundle of deeds and insurance policies that now sat there looked ridiculous.

There had been massive files of ancient documents there when she first became its keeper. She had sent those to the local museum as curiosities. Now the space held only a double handful of folders, on top of which she put the two envelopes with their inscriptions plainly visible.

'If I come through alive, I'll send both to my own lawyer, though even as they are they should stand up in court,' she said aloud. Her voice seemed loud in her own ears. 'If I don't, Evan will open the safe at once, as he has been instructed to do in the event of any emergency. I need not worry about that. But God, if what I fear is true, don't make me have to live with it!' She hadn't realized she was praying until she stopped speaking.

She pushed the heavy door shut, spun

the dials, and left the room. It was time to build up her strength for the thing she felt coming, so she went to the kitchen, heated canned soup, opened crackers. She wasn't hungry, but she felt convinced that before the night was over she might need all her energy.

Then she made coffee and put it in a Thermos. She brought out cookies left from Evan's last visit and put them into a canister, which she tucked under her arm. Cups and spoons, sugar . . . she packed them into a small basket with napkins.

Her heart had begun to race, thudding with dread or excitement or fear, she wasn't sure which. Basket in hand, she went up the stairs to the first landing. Then she paused and set her burdens down.

'I almost forgot,' she exclaimed, feeling in the pocket of her jumpsuit for her keys. Hurrying down again, she unlocked the front door and went out onto the entry porch for the first time in years. The night air was warm and humid, but it seemed intoxicating.

For ten years she had not set her foot

on the steps or the walk beyond them. She touched the iron gate. Then she set her own key in its lock and turned it gently, silently, and heard the tumblers move smoothly to unlock the stout barrier. She didn't push it open but left it, held shut by the latch.

She cocked her head to stare at the sky, which still held a trace of light in the west, although it was somewhere near nine o'clock. A faint smear of stars was visible, even through the reflected lights of the town. A breeze rustled down the street, moving the stiff crepe myrtles that gave it its name.

Marise felt suddenly giddy with this sudden freedom from the confinement of those stone walls. She felt as if she had dissolved into the night and the breeze and the asphalt scented air.

Now that she was outside, she hated to return through the carved door into the musty space of the house. She knew she must, for her duty lay there, for as long as she was alive to perform it.

She turned, her steps slow and reluctant. The thud of the closing door behind her gave her a feeling of entrapment she had thought lost, years before, when she chose this strange imprisonment. She stood for a moment in the entry hall, remembering once again her arrival there.

It had not changed, though the carpet was a bit worn, perhaps, the paint now less than fresh. But the mirror in the hall tree winked in the light of the overhead fixture as she moved toward it and bent to peer into the clouded glass. The fairy forest was still there, blurred into the old mercury of the backing. Her face stared back at her, its lines of strain and age erased in that magical mirror.

'Ben!' The name was jerked from her, but she closed her eyes, held her breath and endured until the need to cry left her.

Marise straightened and went up the stairs, right up, past her waiting basket, her own landing, to the third floor. Down the hall she went, around the turn to Penelope's door, which she had left open on her last visit. The flower basket lamps were bright enough to show her the way as she examined the bolts, the sockets into which they slid, and the lock. Nothing had settled out of plumb enough to disengage any of them. They were still capable of securing this prison.

She leaned her head against the wall and now the tears came, but the fit of weeping was short. She straightened, listening. Had there been a sound below?

No, it was too early. Traffic still moved on the street. Young people zipped past in cars, their radios so loud she could hear them even inside her stone walls. He wouldn't come yet. Not before midnight, she felt with strange certainty.

She knew now that she should have cleaned these rooms, as well as those below, but she hadn't been able to force herself past the door. It might not — surely it would not! — be used at all. This was just an aberration of her own that made her consider such a use to be possible. She had to be wrong.

Suddenly she yawned. She was exhausted, and there would be time to sleep before anything would happen. She could set her alarm, so as to wake in time.

It didn't occur to her as she went back

down, got her basket, and entered her own quarters, that to be able to sleep at such a time was not truly sane.

★ ★ ★

He waited impatiently as the evening dragged past. Once in a while his landlady came to his door with offers of hot tea or cough syrup, and her good intentions irritated him past bearing. He managed to sound properly grateful and hoarse and sleepy, and at last she left him alone.

People wandered in and out until it seemed the house had to be some sort of way station for all restless souls. He ground his teeth.

Eleven o'clock came at last. Eleven-thirty. Don Glass would be coming back at about one, he thought, unless there was some sort of emergency. The watcher wanted to wait for him to come, for if he took his medicine from the policeman's hand it would be proof he had been here all night.

Midnight came. The traffic in the halls

and on the stairs began to slow. By twelve-thirty, things were quiet. At a quarter of one there was no sound in the house at all, except for a relentless mouse between the walls.

He dared not wait much longer to leave. If he missed Glass, so be it. He cracked the door and peered sideways down the hall. Only the dim nightlight could be seen. Nobody was about. He slipped out of his door and padded softly in his sneakers to the head of the stair. Nobody at all was in sight, and he sighed.

He drifted like a shadow down the steep flight of steps, his slender figure in its dark T-shirt and jeans blending into the dimness at the foot of the stair. The entry hall held a ten watt bulb in its six-bulb fixture.

The street was quiet, but he would not risk going out that way. Instead, he crept along the hall to the rear of the house. The back door had, he had discovered long since, a spring lock that snapped automatically. He used it, locking himself out into the warm, exhaust-smelling night.

He moved through the back garden into the long space behind the line of big houses and vacant lots where others had stood in the past. He went into the weed-grown area that had been cow pastures and truck farms, back when the first of these old homes had been built. Now it was the Little League field, and it had been recently mowed.

The Watcher kept clear of the rear fences of those houses that were occupied, for he wanted no dogs announcing his passing. The distinctive shape of the tower against the pinkish glow on a layer of high cloud guided him toward his goal. There was a light in the lower tower room. The sitting room study.

His lips pulled taut in an unconscious grin. He slipped through the vacant lot where his hideout had been. He'd policed that carefully, the day before, and now he passed it without further thought.

Now he was on the sidewalk, beside the iron fence. He followed it silently to the gate, his key in his hand. He couldn't even recall, any longer, how he had come by the key.

He slid the metal shaft into the lock and turned it softly. Then he pushed at the gate, but it didn't move. Panic rose in him. It had to work! He had seen the postman open this gate with this key every day for a week, and it was the only key of its kind he had. It simply had to work!

He turned it again, and the gate opened. It was a moment before he realized what that could mean. He paused, his hand on the gate's flowery grillwork.

It had not been locked . . . something thudded inside his chest. That gate was always locked. Even by day, and without fail every night. Who had left it open? And why?

Was this some sort of a trap?

All those years of deceit, of hiding and moving and avoiding the past, now made him wary. Something smelled wrong. The house waited, dark and enigmatic, while he made up his mind.

He had waited for so long, working and being patient and making his plans for years and years. He could not give it all up now. She was already primed for this night; his letter had seen to that. Whatever came, he had to carry on.

He knew just the cellar window he could force to get into the house. He closed the gate behind him and cut around to the rear of the place. It never occurred to him to try the front door.

He carried a jimmy in his pocket, especially for forcing windows. Burglary had paid his way for much of his life. He knew how to get into any sort of house in the quietest manner possible, and this time was no different. He dropped into the basement at the very back of the house two minutes after he came through the gate.

His tiny flash guided him through the cobwebby space. There was a door, but it was closed. That must be to the apartment in the basement. It had been open before, he thought — but he wouldn't think of that now.

He went past it to the other door opening into the basement hall. Going up the stair in a rush, he found the night light glowing above, lighting the entry hall. He set his feet softly on the steps, the carpet feeling like velvet underfoot.

Then he stopped. No, he would not creep up like a thief. He wanted her to know he was coming, to dread every step, every inch of his progress upward. His lips pulled back again, and he thumped his foot on the carpet. Again and again he stamped on the stairs. He savored every slow, deliberate step.

He pictured her there in her tower room, cowering against the wall, perhaps? Pale, shivering, her narrow hands trembling. Maybe she held a weapon . . . he hoped she did, for it would make it real and exciting. To kill a frightened rabbit would be no sport at all.

But he loved to kill a struggling cat that could threaten him with sharp claws and angry hisses. Such a victory was tremendously satisfying.

He rounded the landing. Pausing, he looked up the corridor, seeing the flower basket lights glowing dimly. There was no dust here. No cobwebs. He'd hoped she was trapped here in a sort of haunted house, surrounded by guilty memories.

He should have known better. She was strong. His own recollections told him so.

And he had been told it by another too.

That would make it even more satisfactory. He felt in his pocket and found his long knife there, sharp in its leather scabbard. It was a useful tool, and he had used it well on more than one occasion.

If she fought, he would feel he truly had the revenge he had dreamed of for so long. A sob of breath came from his throat, surprising him.

He paused, breathing deeply. He must not let himself get all worked up. That led to mistakes. He couldn't afford any of those tonight. He had to do his work here, get back to his room, and be totally unsuspicious to any probing eye.

The single time he'd let his emotions get away from him he had come perilously close to being caught. That mustn't happen tonight.

His heart steadied and he went on, stamping his feet firmly. She must be frantic, he thought.

The half landing was on his right. He touched the doorknob leading into her sitting room, though he knew it would be locked. But the handle turned easily, and the door opened without any effort on his part.

'Come in, Benjie,' said his mother.

★ ★ ★

Marise had slept deeply, as if having this last gnawing question answered had given something inside her release. Only her alarm, which waked her at midnight, kept her from sleeping through until morning. But she rose and entered the sitting room where she moved her small table out from the wall, setting onto it two cups and saucers, spoons, and a bud vase holding a late rose.

When the sound of his feet moved onto the stair, she smoothed her hair and looked about her room. She gave one last touch to the table. She felt nervous but contained.

The opening of the door set her heart fluttering, but by then she sat in her rocking chair, composed, her voice quiet when she invited him in. He stood in the doorway, his stance wary and somehow dangerous. She knew those signs. She had seen them before in her son's aunt. 'Come and sit down. I have coffee and cookies. We have to talk, son.'

His gaze strayed over the room as if in search of some kind of ambush. She knew what he feared, and she said, 'Nobody is here except me. Believe that, Benjie. Come, sit here in Ben's chair. There is no trap here, whatever you may think.'

He sidled into the room and pounced into the angle behind the door. When he found nothing there he moved like some jungle predator toward the chair. She tried to smile, but gave it up as he slipped cautiously into the seat opposite her at the table.

'Coffee?' It might have been any cozy get-together between mother and son. To someone looking in from the outside, it would seem quite natural, the son sitting there quite calmly, Mama with cookies on the table.

'No.' His voice was husky, as if he couldn't quite trust it.

She gazed at him and he stared back. Then he glanced aside at the painting she had put down here that evening. His black eyes narrowed.

'You knew!' he accused her. 'She painted it, and you knew.'

'Not until very recently. Until earlier this week, I hadn't been into Penelope's rooms since that terrible day. Even after I found the portrait, I didn't put it all together. You see, I thought you were dead too. Not until you stepped through the door did I know, with complete certainty, that it was you who let her in that night. You had probably been letting her out of her room at other times. Your father never did figure it out, and for that I am devoutly grateful.'

He was watching her, his face set and pale, his eyes alert for danger.

'It was you, wasn't it? Or did you just run, terrified at what you heard from Aunt Lina's room? Tell me that was it, and I will believe you. It's what I want to believe, just as Evan and the police wanted to. They've been looking for you ever since, and I only just now learned that as well.'

She poured coffee into his cup and put

a cookie on the edge of his saucer. 'Tell me you were out of your mind with fear. I want to hear you say it.'

He laughed, then, doubling over with mirth. That made him bump the table and slosh coffee into the saucer, where it soaked into the cookie.

'You are incredible,' he managed to say at last, though he was still hiccupping giggles. 'You know damn well that I was the one. I visited Pen regularly, even before the day when you caught me up there.' His smile was horrible.

'I'd sneak out of my room at night and go up and let myself in, after I got the key out of your desk. I knew very early there was something in that room I had to know about, and I got the key copied at a key shop near the school. Nobody ever suspects a little kid sent on an errand for his mother, you know. We had some wild times up there, just the two of us.

'But the lot of you kept catching her and locking her up. You even changed locks on us a couple of times, but I always managed to get another key. And she told me everything. The truth about you and

Aunt Lina. About her mother and Miss Edenson.

'Everyone was always against her. They hated her because she was brighter, braver, better than any of them. And then you came, and things got worse for her. You took her twin away from her. She told me that lie you got them to believe about saving my father's life.' He glared at her and she could see the madness well up in his eyes.

'But you didn't keep him from dying. I saw that with my own eyes, right here in this house. The lie was just something you used to get into their good graces, and they fell for you, like a bunch of fools.'

Marise made a protesting sound, and he grinned at her savagely.

'I fell for it too, for entirely too long. You were my mother. I loved you until Pen made me see what you really were. Always the good little woman, busy as a bee managing the farm and doing things around the house and taking care of people, weren't you? But you kept turning everybody further and further away from Pen. She saw it, and once I knew how to look I saw it too.'

'So you turned her loose, thereby killing your Uncle Hannibal, your grandfather, your grandmother, and, I suspect, Miss Edenson too. You were too young to know what she was capable of doing,' Marise said. She felt almost disembodied as her worst imaginings came into being.

His laugh sounded genuinely amused. 'She told Uncle Hanni that I let her loose and she gave him a bit of what she was teaching me. He died before he could say or do anything about it. She gave Grampa that shot, but I tended to Grandmother. I went in and told her what a nasty, smelly, horrible old monster she was.' He snickered.

'She looked at me — you just can't imagine how she looked at me. Then she yelled, 'No! No!' and then she died. And I liked it. So after that I put the medicine into Miss Edenson's milk. She watched me too much, and Pen told me how to do it and where to find the medicine. She prowled around the house a lot more than any of you ever suspected.'

Marise took a gulp of coffee, which was

cooling and very bitter. But it was better than shouting or screaming.

'And then you killed my father. Pen nearly went wild because you wouldn't put him in the hospital. You didn't do a thing to keep him alive, and he just kept getting weaker and thinner, and paler and sicker. I'd go up and cry in her lap, and she'd cry with me. We hated you and hated you and wanted you dead.

'She told me what she planned to do at the funeral. I gave her a map of the woods I drew myself and told her how to get back to the house without being seen using the streets. I took the keys off your desk and opened the gate. I was waiting at the front door when she came.' He took up a cookie and nibbled it absently, as if caught up in the past he was reliving.

'Hildy must have heard us. She called up from her apartment, and we went right down. Pen wouldn't let me come in, and when she came out she was all bloody. I could see red all over the floor, too. She took my hand and we went up to see Aunt Lina.'

He smiled, his eyes bright and black. 'I

helped with that, you know. And after she was dead I helped with the . . . rest of it. I got a little messy too.

'But we couldn't find you. We looked everywhere, downstairs and upstairs, and you weren't even in the tower, so she finally went in there and waited for you. I went back to my room to get my sneakers, and then I waited with Aunt Lina.

'When I came out again, you had come down here and Pen was with you. I could hear from upstairs. And you killed her. Killed Pen! If you could do that, I knew I was too little to handle you. So I ran out, up the road. There was a truck parked at the Mobile station over on Gladder Street, and I crawled into the back with a lot of furniture and pulled the tarp down tight. When we stopped for good we were in Albuquerque.'

So that was how he managed to disappear so thoroughly. Even the driver had probably never known he was there.

'I got out without being seen, and there I was. No clothes, no money, no parents, covered with blood. It was easy to convince the police I couldn't remember anything. They looked for the wreck that had to have happened to me for weeks.

'I grew up in about seven foster homes. They'd get tired of me, after a while, every time.'

Marise could imagine why. She set her cup meticulously in its saucer. 'And all those years you were just waiting to get big enough to come back and kill your mother,' she said in her calmest tone.

'Here I am. Here you are. I won't try to convince you of anything. If you didn't see the true state of affairs when it was before your eyes, you won't believe it now. If you believed the ravings of a madwoman instead of the honest, loving lives of your people, you were already tainted with the flaw that ruined her life. But I must admit it didn't show. You can congratulate yourself on being a very fine actor.'

He glanced up sharply and down again, listening without comment.

'Nobody suspected, once you arrived so healthy and bright, that the Clarrington madness was in you. We thought we'd beaten the odds.' She began to laugh, but there was no amusement in the sound.

The black eyes snapped cold fire. 'Don't try to trick me. I know what I know. We've talked for long enough. I have waited a very long time for this. Why don't I feel excited any more?'

'Because, my poor son, you are quite mad,' she said. The knife caught her under the ribcage, slowing her own movement. But not enough. She pulled her small automatic from the cushion behind her and fired it, point blank, into his face.

His blood and brains spattered the table, the chair, and her jumpsuit with color. Marise gasped. The knife had pulled out of her body at his reflexive jerk. Blood was oozing in a warm flood down her side. With a terrible effort, she pulled herself up and stood swaying over the body of her son.

'God send you peace, Benjie,' she said.

She staggered through the door, across the half landing, onto the stair. The front door loomed near its foot, distant as Everest. With terrible peasant toughness, she set her foot on the step. Clinging to the banister, she struggled downward, kept from falling by her will alone.

The door was nearer. She was almost there, but the light was too dim. She couldn't make out the hall tree. Nothing except the big door.

Then it, too, grew misty. She fell to her knees on the velvet rug at the bottom of the steps. Her hands moved toward the door, as if with a life of their own.

Then they drooped and went still. Not even the sound of her breathing interrupted the quiet.

★　★　★

Evan had not slept well. The memory of that interview with Marise had haunted his dreams, distorted and filled with nightmarish images. Finally, when dawn touched the east, he gave up trying to sleep and went into his small kitchen to make coffee.

This was Saturday. There was no work today to distract him from his unease, nothing planned except perhaps golf at two o'clock with a couple of the Board members. That left the morning completely unoccupied.

He knew before the sun was well up that he was going to visit Marise. The reason, of course, was his need to replace Gertrude Fisk. He kept telling himself that as he got ready, but he kept seeing the thoughtful tilt of Marise's fair head, the evasive expression on her narrow face.

Something was wrong. Badly wrong, if his instinct was right. He wouldn't have a moment's ease until he had made her tell him what that might be. He put on his loafers, got his wallet, and walked quickly away from the house into the freshness of the morning. Already it promised to be hot.

If Marise wasn't up yet, he would wait. The walk would give her time to wake and drink her coffee, he hoped, and the exercise seemed to calm his nerves.

His impatient feet drove his long legs more quickly than he had intended, and the half mile through the shady streets went faster than he'd planned. Before the sun was much higher he was in front of the granite structure. It was too early, and he knew it, but he shook the gate impatiently anyway.

The ironwork opened to his shove.

Something cold and deadly chilled beneath his breastbone. He moved up the walk and the steps to the front door and tried it. His hand was shaking by now.

It, too, moved without hesitation. Evan felt sick dread rise in him, but he pushed the door wide open and let the pale morning light fall across the hardwood floor and the velvety carpet of the entry hall.

Marise lay between the foot of the stair and the door, her hand stretched forward as if she had been reaching for help or safety. When he touched her arm, she was cold and stiff. Her dark jumpsuit was patterned with splotches of rusty blood, which stained the little rug with bright patches.

Evan stared upward, knowing she must have come down the stair. Those blotches of blood were clearly visible on every step.

Would he never finish making terrible discoveries in this house? He looked back down at the dead woman at his feet. Then he stepped around her, very gently, and climbed toward her tower sitting room.

A man lay there, and for a bit he couldn't think who this might be. The face had been shattered by the bullet that killed him, but the eyes were open. Black eyes. Like Ben Clarrington's.

The portrait on the wall told Evan more. Marise had known or suspected something dreadful. The letter — she must have realized, once he told her Benjie's body had not been found, that it could come only from her son.

It was logical, and he was proud of being able to think rationally when he wanted to scream and weep and beat his fists against the pale paper of the walls. He would never know if his guess was accurate, but it satisfied him. Marise would never have protected any murderer except her son.

He made his way down again, averting his eyes from the pitiful body on the rug. Her strictest rule had been that at once, if she died, he was to look into the safe in the study. Obediently, he went there and dug into his wallet for the combination.

The envelope was impossible to miss. She had known this was likely to happen, and she had spent her last hours safeguarding her heritage. He took the envelope, as well as the deeds and insurance policies in the folders.

Then he went into the hall again and looked about him. He could see her there in a hundred ways, bringing tea and cookies, welcoming him into the house, peering wistfully after him as he left.

Evan knew he could not leave her here to be handled and measured by police, for reporters to gnaw to the bone and scandal to overcome at last. He took his lighter from his pocket and touched the flame to the hangings that hid the dining room door. The old fabric blazed up hungrily.

He bent and touched one of those cold hands. 'Goodbye, my dear. God bless,' he said. Then he turned and went out, closing the door behind him.

He locked the gate as well. The street was empty, which was good. He squared his shoulders and walked away from the Clarrington house for the last time.

Evan didn't look back. Already he could

hear the snap of greedy flames as they ate away at the prison in which Marise had lived and died. Let the heritage end, he thought. The final drop of blood is spilled, and the old Clarrington greed is satisfied at last.

THE END

We do hope that you have enjoyed reading this large print book.

Did you know that all of our titles are available for purchase?

We publish a wide range of high quality large print books including:
Romances, Mysteries, Classics
General Fiction
Non Fiction and Westerns

Special interest titles available in large print are:
The Little Oxford Dictionary
Music Book, Song Book
Hymn Book, Service Book

Also available from us courtesy of Oxford University Press:
Young Readers' Dictionary
(large print edition)
Young Readers' Thesaurus
(large print edition)

For further information or a free brochure, please contact us at:
Ulverscroft Large Print Books Ltd.,
The Green, Bradgate Road, Anstey,
Leicester, LE7 7FU, England.
Tel: (00 44) 0116 236 4325
Fax: (00 44) 0116 234 0205